THE FLOWER OF LIFE

by

THOMAS BURKE

1929

British Library Cataloguing-in-Publication Data
A catalogue record for this book is available from the
British Library

Thomas Burke

Thomas Burke was born in Clapham, London in 1886. His father died when he was very young, and at the age of ten he was removed to a home for middle-class boys who were "respectably descended but without adequate means to their support." Burke published his first piece of writing – a short story entitled 'The Bellamy Diamonds' – in 1901, when he was just fifteen. However, proper recognition came in 1916, with the publication of *Limehouse Nights,* a collection of melodramatic short stories set amongst the immigrant population of London's Chinatown. *Limehouse Nights* was serialized in three British periodicals, *The English Review, Colour* and *The New Witness,* and received positive attention from reviewers and a number of authors, including H. G. Wells. It also sparked something of a controversy, however, and was initially banned by libraries due to the scandalous interracial relationships it portrayed between Chinese men and white women.

It was these portrayals of London's Chinatown that Burke is best-remembered for. However, there is some degree of confusion over how much of Burke's writing was based in fact; as literary critic Anne Witchard states, most of what we know about Burke's life is based on works that "purport to be autobiographical, yet contain far more invention than truth." Whatever the truth, there is no doubt that, in his day, Burke was regarded as the foremost chronicler of London's Chinatown at the turn-of-the-century. Burke told newspaper journalists that he had "sat at the feet of Chinese philosophers who kept opium dens to learn from the lips that could frame only broken English, the secrets, good and evil, of the mysterious East," and these journalists almost uniformly took him at his word.

Burke continued to use descriptions of urban London life as a focus of his writing throughout his life. Off the back of *Limehouse Nights*, Burke published the thematically similar *Twinkletoes* in 1918, and *More Limehouse Nights* in 1921. However, he was a prolific author who tried his hand at a number of different genres. He semi-regularly published essays on the London environment, including pieces such as 'The Real East End' and 'London in My Times', and during the thirties even tried his hand at horror fiction. Indeed, in 1949, shortly after his death, Burke's short story 'The Hands of Ottermole' was voted the best mystery of all time by critics. Burke also influenced the burgeoning film industry in Hollywood; D W Griffith, for example, used the short story 'The Chink and the Child' from *Limehouse Nights* (1917) as basis for his silent movie, *Broken Blossoms* (1919), and Charlie Chaplin derived 'A Dog's Life' (1918) from the same book.

THE FLOWER OF LIFE

I.

THEY never saw the green of the trees or the glitter of the stars. They had not the spirit to lift their heads so high. They saw only the flint face of their prison and the meagre gravel of the yard. They knew every line of every feature of that face, and every rain-filled hollow of the yard. They were the defeated, parading in chainless captivity to the glory of life, their conqueror. Their sullen suits were a rebuke to the high morning sun.

To the gates of the workhouse came a little troubled company of surrender. Its units gathered about an old grey woman in cape and bonnet. She carried a tin box. This tin box was all that was left of the castle that she had won from life and lost. She carried it as men carry food in a city stricken with famine.

The women with her were the escort to her surrender. They were delivering her as their

B

hostage to almighty life, and their attitude expressed profound sympathy with her situation. The profound sympathy was tinct with a demure relish that the situation was hers and not theirs, and the relish was poisoned by a spot of fear that it might be.

They hovered about her, anxious to do things and say things that would make the portentous moment casual. They made foolish and futile essays at kindness, knowing that they were foolish and futile, and the old woman saw the folly and futility and gave it the acknowledgment due to sagacity. Her lips talked brightly of common things while her soul sought about for its armour. She was to leave them in the midst of life and take her place inside the gates with the defeated. The moment between the two worlds was as bleak and lonely as the prospect of death.

She turned to them, and gave quick nods of the head to each. Between her and them a race of mental pictures made a moment's flash of colour. The worn flower on her bonnet nodded and drooped like the doffed plume of the vanquished.

"Well . . ."

2.

WHEN the little grey woman was ten years old she was living in a court off Rosoman Street, which is a part of Clerkenwell.

Rudy's Court was the kind of place that looks far more like hell on a summer morning than it does on the blackest midnight. She lived in a world of commination and litany. From every house in the court came complaint, threat, appeal, wrangle and reprisal. Voices held always the tones of anger, but the people were not angry. These tones ruled all their civil intercourse. Under anger they became elaborately dumb.

Her own home was much like the others. Her mother was dead, and an unmarried aunt kept house for her and her father. She kept it bitterly and clamantly, and she gave Jane a share of the keeping. All her life Jane's mind echoed sentences that echoed her first memory of life.

"Now then, you Jane—sweep them stairs, and don't take all day over it."—"Now, you Jane, run round to Posgate's and get me a packet of candles. And don't stop jawing with them Martin gels. Else I'll wallop you."—"Go out

3

playing? What next? When there's the bed-room to be turned out."—"Don't you pout at me, me lady, else I'll give you what-for."

The jutting fact about the court was not its dirt or its clamour, but its piety. All its people attended church or chapel. Out of their dog-kennels and their darkness they praised God as though he had given them Park Lane. Their attitude of submission seemed to say that it was only in His marvellous mercy that He didn't blast them utterly. All current faiths had their adherents, and dispute and defence of them served the clamour when other causes waned. They measured the supremacy of their faith by the teas and the outings it afforded. Some were so pious that they attended three churches and reconciled three conflicting creeds. They had blankets and groceries and coals from one, magic-lantern shows from another, and summer outings from a third. By these literal means the church hoped to prove to them the efficacy of belief.

Her aunt had made a close study of the local churches and their recognition of piety. It had been close, because a natural integrity compelled her to give her faith once and for all. After some thought she had chosen St. Peter's as offer-ing the most steady return, and she shut her ears to all talk of benefits to be had by occasional patronage of other saints, and set an example by single loyalty to St. Peter.

So Jane went to daily school at the St. Peter's Church Schools, and to the Band of Hope and Sunday School of the same foundation. She learnt reading, writing and simple arithmetic, and a little history and geography. The chief training was in those useful matters that would fit her for service in the station of life to which it had pleased God to call her.

At the Band of Hope on Wednesday evenings she sang songs that she didn't understand about the splendour of water and the devilry of strong drink. These songs were sung to the airs of English drinking songs. They told her stories about drunkards that were more thrilling than any fairy-tale. They showed her coloured charts of the stomach, and demonstrated the miserable end of a blue-bottle when it fell into whisky. At Christmas they gave her a tea, followed by games and a cantata, and a bun and orange to take home. In the summer they gave her an outing to Highgate Woods, with threepence to spend.

The Sunday School teachers trained her into a blind acceptance of Jewish and Syrian fable; the acceptance helped her to live kindly and bravely. They supported her in her faith by a similar Christmas tea and a similar summer outing; and they rewarded her punctual and regular attendance by prizes of deeply religious books. In these books the heroine was always a girl of the labouring classes. The girl worked hard and lived the religious life in face of the jeers of her comrades. She won a steady husband, a tidy cottage, and healthy children. Her irreligious comrades went by numbers into the workhouse or the hospital. Jane read these tales and abided by them.

Her aunt was a chilblain on the skin of life. Her father was its balm. He held towards her that attitude of heavy facetiousness by which the uneducated disguise their affections. She thought this funny, and enjoyed it. He called her Shrimp, and spoke of having her for tea one day. He calculated that it would take forty of her to make a penn'orth. He warned her to be careful when she was coming home from Sunday School, because Sunday afternoon was the time when people bought shrimps. He was full of this drollery. His sister sniffed at it.

He had great tales of the days when he was in the Navy. Jane had heard the whole six of them a hundred times, but she was always ready to hear them again. They showed her father as cunning, and brave, and noble, and gentle, and jocular; and as big a fool as the next man. He was hero

6

and victim and villain. It was fine to have such an all-round fellow for father. She compared him with other fathers in the court. The comparison created clear excuses for their daughters.

Her days revolved around his return from work. His first glance and word were for her. To him it was a ritual: to her it was an event. In the summer she went to meet him at the corner. In the winter she waited for him at the door. Years later, when she thought of her father, she thought of the tender lamplight of Rosoman Street; of Saturday afternoons of December when lavender mist made the court an isolated star; of the firelit kitchen, and drawn blinds shutting them from the shrill doorways; and of dripping-toast for tea. Saturday afternoon and evening made a sort of weekly Christmas Day. Father then was free and unbuttoned, and there was always dripping-toast for tea. At tea-time he was up to his larks, and if Aunt Sophy sniffed, her sniffs hadn't the power they had on other evenings. Or on Sundays.

Sunday wasn't at all a good day. He was at home, but she had less of his company than on week-days. He made the day a debauch of sleep, and the cottage was an effervescence of sniffs. He had breakfast in bed. After breakfast he turned under the bed-clothes. Aunt and Jane went to church, and Jane took the dinner to the bake-house before church, and collected it after church. He was up for dinner, but only half-awake. After dinner he went to sleep again. Jane went to Sunday School. At tea-time he woke up with a noise like M-yuua, and gave his mind to winkles and watercress and tea. He asked questions about Sunday School, but his Sunday tone was not his weekday tone. Jane felt that he wasn't really listening. He was a genial porcupine, and the potential bristles defeated the geniality. After tea Aunt Sophy went to evening service, and Father attended lectures at a workingmen's institute, or went for a walk. Jane was left at home with orders to keep an eye on everything, to lay the supper, and to go to bed at eight o'clock. She could cut herself a slice of bread-and-butter before she went to bed. She went to bed at eight, and was always awakened at ten. It was only on Sundays that Father kicked the doorstep.

Childhood, like most truly-remembered child-hoods, was one long boredom, lit here and there by burning patches of adventure and calamity.

Adventure swooped upon her in Farringdon Road. She was coming home from afternoon school, and midway was seized by a great hawk. The hawk had long thin legs. Its crest was a silk hat that rode on half the head. Its wings were the flaps of an Inverness cape. Its talons and its mouth were ferocious, but its glittering eyes were kind. In one of the eyes it held a piece of glass. Its mate, looking something like an owl, addressed it as Jimmy. A lean talon shot to Jane's shoulder, and the thing spoke to her in human language. It said: "Where do you live, child? Take me to your mother."

She said: "Please, sir, I live in Rudy's Court in Rosoman Street. And I haven't got a mother."

Hawk said: "Well, what *have* you got? Every child's got *something*."

She said: "I live with Father and Aunt Sophy."

He said: "Then take my hand and lead me to one of 'em."

So, although she was frightened, she took the hawk's talon, and started to lead him to Rosoman Street. But by the time they had crossed Farringdon Road she wasn't frightened any more: he said such funny things. At a sweet-shop he sent the owl to buy her a big threepenny prize-packet, and then, although she had told him her name was Jane Cameron, he called her Macduff, and told her to lay on.

When they came to Rudy's Court she called

Aunt Sophy, and told her a gentleman wanted to see her. Aunt Sophy came out, and she and the hawk had some chat. What it was about Jane couldn't guess, but as he kept saying she must sit, she thought he must be a doctor or someone from the school. She didn't want to sit. On Sundays Aunt was always telling her to sit down when she wanted to stand or move about. But at last Aunt said Yes, that would be all right; and the hawk and the owl went away. Aunt told her that he was a man who painted pictures, and that she was to go to his house after school, and sit down while he painted a picture of her.

So, on three afternoons of that June, Aunt met her at the school gate, and they went for a long ride by omnibus to the house where the artist lived. It was near the river. And when they got there, she didn't have to sit at all. She had to stand against a mirror, and look at the hawk. He had no wings this time. He was dressed like a Smithfield porter. He wore a long blue smock.

He wasn't so funny at home as he had been outdoors. He was like Aunt Sophy. He buzzed and flapped. He kept telling her to keep still and hold her head up, child. For goodness' sake, couldn't she keep her head up?

At the end of each afternoon he gave her some

oranges, and on the third afternoon he gave Aunt some money, and told her she would see it in the autumn.

In September Father and Aunt took her with them one Saturday afternoon to the West End, and they went into a big building in Bond Street. And there, hanging on the wall among a lot of other pictures, all in beautiful gold frames, was herself. Herself in pork-pie hat, blue cotton coat, white stockings with black hoops, and spring-side boots; herself standing against a mirror—where another herself, much fainter, was shown —looking straight out at everybody. It wasn't what you could call a coloured picture : it was all dark blue and dirty white; but it was herself. It said so. It was labelled " Jane."

Father said that his Jane had now been immortalised, but she didn't understand him.

That was the adventure. The calamity fell in the next year. It was Christmas-time, and a newly-opened shop in Sullivan Street was attracting custom by a new trick. It was presenting coloured air-balloons to children whose parents spent two shillings. Not merely red balloons or green balloons or blue balloons, but balloons striped with every colour you knew. She had looked with white eyes at boys and girls carrying these dancing blossoms, and all her evening talks with Father had the word Balloon in them.

At the end of a week when he had done much over-time, he promised carnival; and on Saturday evening he allowed her to lead him to the shop. In exchange for his coin he received some socks and a white collar. Jane received the emblem of paradise.

On the way home the dust of Rosoman Street broke into bits of gold. The dull world came to life. Between her and the daily grey swam the balloon. It was her palace window. Through it she saw all things as princesses are thought to see them. It gave her the strength and valour that faith gives to the religious. She fondled it. Secretly she kissed it. Father's voice constantly advised her: " Careful, now. Careful. Hold it tight." She held it very tight.

They were scarcely indoors before she began playing with it. Aunt Sophy said " What's all this nonsense ? " but the radiance of the balloon dulled the sharp words into nothing. In the lamplight it disclosed new wonders. All the colours of the world's gardens bounced and soared and floated about the room. Father said : " Careful, now. Shouldn't play with it too much. Tie it to the back o' that chair. Else you might lose it."

But she couldn't tie it up yet. A lover can't stop touching the hand of his mistress, even in the moment of peril. She went on playing. It swam across the room and lit the air with flames of purple and gold and scarlet. It danced prismatic dances on the back of her hand. It lifted an everyday kitchen into the transformation-scene of pantomime. It brought something very like God very near to her. Her eyes were hot with adoration of its beauty.

Father said : " Now, that's enough for to-night. Tie it up."

" Oh, just once more ! "

And then, on the pat of a finger, and before Father had said more than one word of " Look out for the fire ! " the angel of the Lord had fled. It sailed sweetly across the room. Then it lost itself and plunged down the air-way to the alluring coke.

The faintest pop marked the passing of glory and loveliness. It had been there. It was not there.

For a second Jane stared at the red hell that had devoured her angel. Then she bowed over the table. Her howls were heard across the court.

That night, because it was Christmas-week, the supper was luxury. There was fried bacon. Jane ate none of it.

Before she was old she was to know much pain and to lose other beautiful things. But never did she know again the pain of that night. Of the many things that she lost, she lost none by deliberate folly.

3.

At fourteen Jane was a nursery-maid. She received eight pounds a year and her keep. She worked hard and lived lavishly on royal foods.

The family had a house in Cavendish Square and a home in Suffolk. In later years Jane would talk of her days at Steeple End as lost spirits might talk of paradise. They were the crescent of ecstasy by which she measured all her stars of delight. She had been lifted from fume and grit into a lustrous confusion of green and gold. Set in this confusion were marvellous people who moved through hours of silk and crystal. She was a Cockney, and she loved London, but amid the green and gold she forswore her birthright.

She first saw Steeple End in April, when its hundreds of acres were a beach of blossom, and the air was tingling with the ardent odours of the spring. Two sides of the Italianate mansion were lapped by a lawn of living velvet. Beyond the lawn was a meadow where daffodils dozed. The house was so open to the sky that all the tides of light beat upon it. Against the blazing pallor of its walls green and yellow were almost black. In the coppice on the eastern side a blue-bell patch threw up such colour that wood-smoke seemed to hover under the trees. Through this smoke the sun sent a quiver of lemon spears. Larks haunted the near wheatfields and all the golden air, and rooks haunted the elms, and blackbirds and thrushes and wagtails flirted about the coppice and the centuried walks.

Life was drenched in sunshine and singing blue. She felt that she must remember for ever the early sun on the daffodils and the choir of larks; but the abiding memory of those days was the smell of cows as they ambled through the meadow at afternoon milking-time. Her mind worked like that. It loved the beautiful and remembered the useful.

After she had tended the day nursery and the night nursery, the babies were in her charge, and through the vibrant morning she toddled them about the lawn. For the rest of the day they were in Nurse's charge, and she was Nurse's servant. It was a solemn office, this care of the beautiful children of her imperial master and mistress, and she performed it with the breathless zeal of one dedicated to the care of relics. It was not servitude, but service. To every detail of her task she brought a warm white essence of reverence. She charged each act of the day with it, as though that were the first and last act that she would do. She was not conscious of this spirit. It sprang from some unperceived cause that had nothing to do with duty to employers or Sunday Schools or natural grace, but perhaps something to do with the babies and the grass and the great house and the singing blue.

Her child's face smiled out of the fetters of age. She wore a stiff black dress to her ankles, white paper cuffs and collar, a white apron and a white cap. Her hair was " up." It was neatly parted and braided, and was packed and netted on the nape of her neck. The thin braids were strung in a loop round her ears, in the style of the times.

She liked her fetters. She thought they helped her to look as mature and serious as she felt. She had no beauty, but her appearance was pleasing. She was as trim as an expert packer's parcel.

She saw little of the rest of the establishment. She and Nurse lived and ate and slept in superior detachment at the top of the house, and only once or twice was she received in the servants' hall. Although she lived in the same house, and sometimes met the housemaids and the footmen on the stairs, she was cut off from them. A visit to them was like a visit to another house. Some

of them, even in four months, she did not see at
all. By being much outdoors with the babies,
she knew best the under-gardener and the groom;
but these were outdoor servants who lived in
their own quarters. They were admitted to the
servants' hall only by courtesy.

Her first visit was as awesome as her first
presentation to her mistress. These people were
fellow-servants of hers, but she was a shy guest
at an august party. She was taken down by
Nurse. They gave her the melted edge of toler-
ance that benign superiors give to their juniors.
The butler made a joke about her size. Cook
nodded to her and looked her over. Only the
kitchen-maid and the tweeney accepted her as an
equal. They told her stories of their homes.

She was not only under the eye of her hosts:
she was under the eye of her immediate officer,
Nurse; and she had to watch herself. The
etiquette was almost royal. She learned from
Nurse that she must not speak to the butler or to
Cook or to the head-parlourmaid, unless she was
spoken to; and then must only answer their
remark. She had no right to make uninvited
conversation. The others she could address freely,
if none of the seniors was speaking. By some
tradition whose purpose was not clear, there were
distinctions in forms of address. Cook had no

name : she was Cook. Nurse and parlour-maids were addressed by surnames—Jordan, Layton, Martin. Housemaids and kitchen juniors were addressed by Christian names. The butler was Vincent; the footmen were Robert and John.

Places at the supper-table were fixed with a nice sense of professional precedence. Cook sat at the head and the butler at the foot. On Cook's right sat the chief parlour-maid, and next her the second parlour-maid. On Cook's left came the upper housemaid, and next her the under-housemaid. On the butler's right the first footman sat, and on his left the second footman. Below them sat the boys, meeting in the middle the junior girls.

The butler carved with exact technique from a master joint. Plates were passed by the pantry-boy and the tweeney. They did their work with the nervous solemnity of students under examination by professors. Manners were closely watched. Whispering or giggling was a breach of decorum. Also scraping the plate with the knife. There was much admonishment. The butler watched the footmen and the boys. Cook watched the girls. From time to time she sent a glance down the table to the scullery-maid or the tweeney, with a sharp "Annie!" or "Emily!" Annie or Emily flushed and froze.

The talk was of things beyond Jane's range. Whether they were going to Cowes in July. Whether they would go to the moors in August. Rumours that they would not. Stories of the bad taste of the rich Sir Harold, who had given the butler a five-pound note for a week-end visit. Of the shocking manners of Lady Pulcrude. Of the new fashion of Scotch whisky, and the displacement of cigars by cigarettes. Of the move to town for the Season. Of Mr. Frank's latest disaster at Oxford. There was no talk of their personal affairs or of general affairs: only of the family's affairs and of happenings in the house. That was their world, and they had no life save in that world. Jane was proud to be in that world, and eager to have a recognised place in it.

They asked for news of the children, and Nurse held their attention for ten minutes. Jane could have told a hundred anecdotes of the children, all better than Nurse's, but nobody asked her. She began to whisper one of them to the kitchen-maid, but the kitchen-maid had an apprehensive eye on Cook, and nudged her to silence.

When Nurse signed to her to come upstairs, she was glad to go, but once she was back in the nursery she felt that she had had a thrilling evening. She thought about it in bed. They had all been very nice to her, and the kitchen-maid was going to be her friend. Life was opening out. It was but one step short of paradise. If only Father could be with her.

She spoke of this to Nurse, and Nurse smiled at the father-worship. But she said that perhaps Father might come down some time just for the day. Jane asked if such a thing could possibly be, and out of her casually generous temperament Nurse promised to speak to Lady Mellonspar about it.

Some weeks later, she happened to remember her promise, and Lady Mellonspar gave permission for the visit. Father got a Saturday off and came down. The groom, by the coachman's permission, drove her in the governess cart to the station, and drove them back. Father had made so much the best of himself that she hardly knew him. He was tidily bright in a suit of grey shoddy and the hard hat of Sundays. He wore a stiff collar without giving notice that it was stiff. He held himself with dignity, but left a little loose button to hint to the groom that he could, on encouragement, burst into good-fellowship. In the day's intercourse he revealed unsuspected stores of knowledge, and he wore manners that Jane, despite her worship, had never credited to him. She had only seen him as a tired workman. She had never seen this man of the world.

Before dinner she showed him her rookery and her bluebell patch and her lawn and her ornamental garden. She told him of her friend, Amy, the kitchen-maid. At tea-time she was allowed to show him her nursery and her babies. He gave Nurse the due respect of her position, and said "Yes, ma'am," "Why, certainly, ma'am." He hoped that Jane served her well, and thanked her for her firmness with Jane, and observed how Jane was profiting in health and character by being in such a good place under such serious training. He was introduced to Master Horace, aged four, and Miss Agatha, aged two. He offered them a fat and respectful finger to shake. Jane showed him her white night nursery, with its rainbow frieze of fairy-tale characters. She identified each of the characters, and explained how Master Horace loved her to tell him their stories.

During nursery tea Lady Mellonspar made one of her rare visits to her children, and Father was presented to her. He made her his best bow, and she gave him gracious recognition. He said nothing but "Yes, m'lady," and "No, m'lady," until she encouraged him to say more. Then he showed that he knew how to talk to the nobility and gentry. She discussed Jane with him as though Jane were her abiding concern. She spoke of Jane's marked success in her situation. She listened to his respectful sentences on the bringing-up of children, and approved his honest attitude to life and his homely wisdom. She told him that a good home made all the difference to a working-girl, and that she knew by Jane's superior ways and speech that she had a good home behind her. That was why she had felt it safe to engage her for such a position of trust. She praised him indirectly by telling Jane that if she attended always to her father's advice she would do very well.

Two days later she passed Jane on the terrace, and asked her what her name was, and how long she had been with them.

All that Saturday he was a success. The builder's office, where he got his day's orders for work, was next door to a livery stable. He thus had enough knowledge of horses to put himself right with the groom. He had a brother who was a gardener. The brother was helpful when the under-gardener magnanimously took him round the hot-houses. He was able to recognise the blooms and to say the right thing about them. With the butler's world he had no contact, but he was a Mason and the butler was a Mason. In the pantry, after dinner, they had affable talk on Masonic and other affairs. The butler told him some stories, and he laughed with a controlled mirth that subtly suggested the strain of controlling it before such assaults of wit. He told some stories to the butler, and the butler went down to the cellar and brought up a bottle, and they made an afternoon of it.

At dinner in the servants' hall he was approved by the Cook for his sense, by the parlour-maid for his manners, and by the younger servants for his humour. He had a "way" with all of them.

As this was a special day, Jane was invited to the dinner. She glowed in the rays of his success. In the evening, when he had gone, the emptiness that his going left with her was filled by their comment.

"Well, Jane, you're lucky to have such a funny father. The things he *says* ! "—" I did like your father, Jane. So nice and gentlemanny."—" I can see now why you're such a good girl, Jane. It's your father."

For two days the stables and the home farm ached with his stories.

They held him until the last up-train, and she was allowed to go with him to the station. The groom and the governess cart again served them. Cook presented him with a roll of the home butter, and the gardener gave him a bag of fresh lettuces and cucumbers, and Jane was told to pick him an armful of bluebells.

They reached the station twenty minutes before the train, and he made a civil offer of hospitality to the groom. The groom accepted, and they went across the road while Jane held the pony. When they came out the groom was laughing with deep country Ho's. Father kissed her three times, and ordered her always to be a good girl, even if she couldn't be a big girl, and reminded her that the little 'uns often turned out to have more in 'em than the big 'uns. Then he punched her between the shoulders and got into the train. He waved a white handkerchief from the window, and she was proud of him. It was just like him to remember to have a *white* handkerchief to wave.

On the drive home through the creeping stillness of the fields the groom broke often into chuckles. His only explanation was: " Your father's a One. Oh, dear ! . . . oh, dear ! "

To every mortal is granted one day that shall hold its diamond sparkle through many years. That was Jane's day.

But nothing good stayed long with her. The coloured balloon had rushed out of her hands before she had realised that it was hers. And the ecstasy of Steeple End was scarcely realised before it was a memory.

In middle May the family went to town, and Nurse and Jane were left with the children. Three other servants stayed to keep the house in order.

The first hint of trouble was given by the gardener. He had had a letter from the butler, and he told Nurse about it. He told her in the centre of the lawn, looking right and left while he talked. What he told her was faint rumour, and by the time it reached Jane it was even fainter. But it could still breathe, and its breath was trouble. The tweeney had overheard Nurse murmuring to the under-housemaid, and could repeat the words, " . . . the City. . . . Nearly everything. . . . Dreadful. . . . Can't go on." Murmuring meant trouble, and trouble could only mean that somebody was going to be discharged.

Through the next week clouds of gloom floated in and out of the shrouded rooms of the house. Nurse dropped her large bright masculine ways and became feminine and testy. She slaughtered all Jane's questions. She pretended not to know what the questions meant, and ordered her tartly not to get silly ideas into her head, and to mind her own business. The gardener and the under-gardener went through the gay mornings with the air of men who have had miserable nights.

26

They snapped Jane's chatter in two. Life in the kitchen was like walking through a strange room in the dark. Throughout the day they bumped against each other. The elders had only a hint of impending disaster, and the two juniors had only a hint that there was a hint. They wanted to know, and the elders rated them for wanting to know, because they, too, wanted to know. Even the babies were peevish.

Within a fortnight they all knew. A solicitor came down and assembled the five indoor servants and the outdoor servants in the dining-room. To each of them he handed the wages that were due as a week's or a month's notice. The gardeners would be kept on until the new owners came in. The grooms and stable-hands would remain until the horses were disposed of. All the rest were dismissed, and must leave the house by Saturday. The head-gardener's wife would act as caretaker.

The groom interpreted the technical jargon as meaning a fair and ruddy crash. He added that he had seen it coming. He offered a graphic sketch of Sir Charles running for his life, and his good lady in lodgings, supporting her children by needlework. He was ordered to cease his blasphemy. He replied that life was life, and facts was facts, and sensible people didn't pretend

27

they wasn't. He was profoundly wise. He wore his wisdom with a tolerant grin.

That night Nurse surrendered her dignity, and she and Jane became comrades in grief. Before the prospect of parting from their babies, they spent the night sobbing on each other's shoulders.

Next day she packed her box and tried to tune her mind to Rosoman Street. The groom got out the governess cart and drove her to the station. As they trotted down the crisp drive she looked back at the house. The cows, heavy with milk, were plodding to the cowshed through the dreaming grass of four o'clock. She looked back and hid her face in her handkerchief. The groom patted her shoulder and told her of his plans for going to Australia.

4.

At nineteen Jane was a drudge. She was
" general " at a pawnshop in Bloomsbury. She
was up at half-past five each morning, and throughout the day she scrubbed and washed and dusted
and cooked and sewed and shopped. She fell
into bed at half-past eleven.

She lived in a square mile whose dominant
note was food. Hardly had the morning air
cleansed itself of the smell of breakfast, when it
was greased with the smell of coming lunch. To
the fading of the smell of lunch came the pungent
support of the smell of a thousand dinners.
Three times a day this business of eating flushed
the lymphatic air with the golden noise of Burma.
Three times a day a thousand gongs sent out their
muezzin-calls to boarding-house meals. Above
this stir the three balls of the House of Lombardy
hung in suspended comment. They, too, had
their part in Bloomsbury's business of eating.
Without their help many meals would have been
missed.

For the rest of her life the sight of those three
balls gave Jane a creeping of the skin. They

hung above the ultimate pit, the grave of respectability. Once one had entered it, one could
never again walk freely in the pure air. The
reek and stain of it clung for years. The people
who came to the little cubicles brought with them
the miasma of defeat, and this miasma oozed from
their bundles in the store-room and crept about
the house. Jane's senses were so keen to that
miasma that she could perceive it in trains and
trams and buses. Some of these people came
regularly, and went about apparently unconscious
of wearing a stigma. She marvelled that they
could look their fellow-creatures in the face.
They must be calloused to all the prickings of
honour and esteem. Their condition was pitiable. It was but one jump short of the infamy
of the street-walker. She prayed that God in
His mercy would save her from becoming like
them.

She never knew how hard she worked, and
never complained. A " place " was a " place,"
and work was work. She did not go to it with
the sullen docility of the slave, or the idiot alacrity
of the soldier, but with the sober vigour of one
discharging an obligation. Her mistress was
large and fleshy, and when kindness cost nothing
she was kind. Her master was thin and foxy
and exacting; these qualities were glazed with

wit and humour. There was a daughter of fifteen. This daughter was of tomboy temperament, and made a playmate of her. In the underground kitchen, between chores, they snatched good times.

The daughter was fond of boys and talked tirelessly of her escapades. Rather than be without boys' company, she was willing to pay for it. A group of lordly lads knew her weakness, and, when meeting her, contrived never to have any pocket-money. They boasted to each other of the sums they had extracted from her.

Jane had no patience with these goings-on. She heard of them with scorn and disgust. She had built around herself a stout wall of prudence, and within it she lived tightly. To venture beyond it meant living thoughtlessly, and thoughtlessness led to gaiety, and gaiety to folly, and folly to trouble and debt and the pawnshop and the workhouse. She had seen it happen. A lot of it had begun by going with boys. She deeply desired her world's respect, and she saw that the way to it was by demure deportment. She could not understand how others could be so loose, and her judgment of these sinners was harsh. Sensible people didn't sin. She could find no excuses for fools. They had all been taught how to behave.

She was still without beauty, but she had an amusing face. People liked to look at it. She had her father's love of waggery, and there was a hint of it in the shape of her mouth. It was her mouth that attracted the butcher's young man, and gave him much misery. He was ardent and patient, and she was fond of him. But he could not move her. She examined the matter from every point of her walled enclosure, and decided that she hadn't yet had enough experience of life. He might turn out well, and then he might not. She had the example of many early marriages to guide her, and she had long seen the folly of yielding to impulse. Rapture to her was light-headedness. Love-making was flummery. By giving way to silly nonsense that belonged to novelettes she might be " had." Young men so often turned out different after marriage; they couldn't be trusted to know their own minds when young. She would wait till she was older, when there would be no danger of being " had."

Her mistress was a little concerned at finding youth so hesitant of romance. She condemned " fast " girls, but she liked girls to be girls and boys to be boys. And if you didn't get a bit of romance when you were young, you never would get it. Anyway, you were only young once, and what was the good of being young if you didn't

get a bit of romance? She thought Jane un-
naturally slow and prim. Her master approved
her sense. He did not like the girl of the period,
and expressed pleasure that Jane was wise enough
not to be in the fashion. She would find the
right sort of husband in good time : a better
husband than romance would find for her. He
spoke from experience of romance. When all
girls were getting out of hand, he thought it
refreshing to find one like Jane. He wished his
daughter would take her as a pattern. His
daughter, behind his back, put out her tongue.

After her first year at the pawnshop the desire
came to her to consolidate her position in life as
a young woman. The consolidation was to take
the form of a black silk dress for Sundays. For
many months her inner life was homage to the
goddess of black silk dresses. Shilling by shilling
and sixpence by sixpence she made votive offering
to it. Far ahead in the calendar stood a Sunday
rippling with emotional banners. On that Sunday
afternoon she would arrive in Rudy's Court and
display to Father her first silk dress.

She was within three months of it when it
slipped from her grasp.

She was busy one morning in the scullery when
she saw the daughter creeping out of the kitchen.
She had not heard her come in, and wondered

why she had been so furtive. Ten minutes later
she knew. Her mistress came in and began to
fuss about the kitchen, and then said : " Have
you seen that half-sovereign I left on this bill ? "

" No, m'm. What bill ? "

More pointedly, and slowly, she said : " I put
half a sovereign on this bill of Truman's. Ten
minutes ago. It's gone."

" I haven't seen it, m'm. I been mangling all
the time. I haven't been in the kitchen."

" Oh. . . . Well, I put it there. I know I put
it there. Only ten minutes ago. It was *there*.
Just in the middle of the bill. I held it there with
my finger while I was thinking. You can see the
mark."

" Well, I haven't seen it, m'm. I been in the
scullery the last half-hour."

" Well, it was there ten minutes ago. And it
isn't there now." She fixed her eyes on Jane
with the cold gaze of suspicion. Under this gaze
Jane became awkward. " Nobody could have
got into the kitchen from the shop. And nobody's
been here but you. So how d'you account for
it ? "

The gaze and the direct question revealed to
Jane the indirect accusation. For a second or so
she fumbled and hesitated. She understood now
the daughter's silent visit to the kitchen : she

remembered the boys who had to be placated. She was innocent, but the sudden charge, and the realisation of her playmate's sin, shocked her into the appearance of guilt. She stammered three words, and her cheeks breathed through fire to ice and ice to fire. Her mistress watched her. "How—I mean—how can I account for it? I don't know nothing about it. I never saw it there at all."

"Well, it *was* there, and it isn't. Things can't run away of their own accord. *Some*body's taken it."

"Well, I haven't taken it, m'm. I should a-thought you knew me well enough for that. I —you—it's wicked to say such a thing."

"I haven't said anything yet, Jane."

"Well, you're trying to. You're going to say I stole it."

"I'm only asking for an explanation."

"Well, I haven't got one."

"Then what can you expect me to think? Here was half a sovereign ten minutes ago. Now it's gone. And nobody here but you."

"I can't help that. I keep telling you I don't know nothing about it. I been in the scullery, mangling."

"Well, who *could* have taken it?"

Jane's hesitation at the question gave strength

to the charge. And when at last she said slowly :
" I don't know," her mistress nodded three
times.

" I see. You can't think of any way it might
have gone ? "

She waited, but Jane said nothing. There
were steps on the basement stairs. The daughter
approached the kitchen door. At sight of her
mother and of the tense attitude of Jane, she
stopped. Her face said that she knew what was
happening.

" What is it, Minnie ? "

" Nothing, Mother. I was only coming to
speak to Jane."

" Well, go away. We're busy."

Jane stopped her. " Mistress says she left half
a sovereign here just now, and it's gone. As
nobody's been in the kitchen she thinks I stole it.
Do you think I stole it ? "

" There's no need to tell Minnie, Jane. We
can settle this ourselves without telling everybody."

Minnie's face was white. Her eyes were frozen.
Jane tried to make her look at her, but she wouldn't.
She waited for her to confess. No confession
came. Minnie looked down at the floor, and
described an arc with the point of her shoe. Her
mother laid her embarrassment to hearing her

playmate charged. "Run away, now, Minnie, Run away."

Minnie lingered. She kept her eyes from the part of the kitchen where Jane stood. Jane was not hating her. She was thinking of her in indignation and contempt. "You poor thing! . . . You poor miserable thing." Minnie knew this. Knew, too, that she was safe; that the strong and self-sufficient Jane would not preserve herself by denouncing her cowardly playmate. She went slowly out of the kitchen and up the dark stairs.

"Well, Jane?"

"There's nothing I can say, m'm. 'Cept that I don't know nothing about it. And it's wicked of you to think it."

"It's still more wicked to steal, Jane. I've always known you to be honest. But I know that none of us is above temptation. Come, now. . . ."

"Steal? *Me!*"

"What else can I think?"

"I don't know. You must think what you like." She was getting angry. "You can search me all over. And me box, too. I know nothing about it."

"Jane!" The tone was suppliant.

"If you choose to think me a thief I can't stop you."

" Well, what can you expect anybody to say if I told them? If I told them that I left half a sovereign in a room where there was only one person, and that when I came back it was gone. What would any common-sense person say?"

" I s'pose they'd say what you say. Just because it looks like that. But it isn't. You don't trouble to think whether it mightn't have fallen off the table."

" It couldn't. I pressed it down on the bill quite hard."

" Well, I was mangling all the time in the scullery. Why don't you find out whether anybody else came in and make sure?"

" Nobody did come in. We know that. Mr. Lane's been in the shop all the morning, and would have seen if anybody tried to slip down."

" How d'you know Minnie mightn't have come down?"

" Minnie's been with me all the morning. What are you—what do you mean about Minnie coming down? Are you trying to suggest——"

" Oh, nothing."

" Jane! Are you trying to shield yourself by——"

" *What?* " Her manner took a sudden flare. She checked it. If she got too angry she might

38

say more than she wanted to say. She told herself that she mustn't say it. "Oh, think what you like. It's useless for me to keep on telling you I never seen your half-sovereign. But that's the truth."

"Oh, Jane, Jane! Look here, I don't want to be hard. I ought not to have left it lying about like that. I know it's temptation. If I find it this afternoon I'll say no more about it."

"*I* can't help you find it. That's a certainty."

Her mistress sighed. "Very well, Jane. If it's like that, we'll have to leave it. I'm not accusing you. But I can't keep you. You must go this afternoon."

"Go? You really think—— How dare you——" She stammered again and went white and red with confusion and disgust. She knew that she could save herself by telling the truth, and she knew that if she saved herself by telling the truth she would never be happy again. They had been such friends. She could not complete her sentences. Her demeanour fully convinced her mistress. It was the blustering demeanour that would have convinced anybody.

"Yes, you must go. Unless——"

"Oh, I'm sick of it. Be quiet. Be quiet. I can't say more than I've said. I never seen it.

39

And you can search me all over. And now be quiet. I'll go."

That afternoon Jane arrived in Rudy's Court with her box and without a " reference." She did not get her silk dress that year nor the next. Father never saw her in a silk dress.

5.

THE great cranes on the peaks of the tripod scaffolds made a string of delta on the palimpsest of the sky. In the hard light of the January afternoon they seemed charged with meaning. They blazed over the townscape like an occult proclamation from a race of giants.

But as the fingers of the dusk crept across the face of the city, and changed its features into a quivering nebula, their message faded. They ceased to be symbols. They were only the tools of men. When the dark came they were not even tools. They were nothing.

In the last gasp of light a man moved along one of their platforms. Because he could not see them he had forgotten them, and he moved swiftly and without caution. He reached the edge and looked over and hailed a man on a ladder. The man on the ladder looked up to answer. As he looked up he gave a great cry. The man on the platform bawled " What is it, mate ? " In the next second the rope and cradle of one of the cranes swung inward on its last journey. It missed its point and swung outward

41

again. On its passage out the cradle struck the man in the middle of the back. He appeared to take a considered dive into the air, and then to change his mind. He clutched at projecting beams to stop his dive. In the two-hundred-feet drop he turned over twice. He came down on a cart loaded with raw cement.

At half-past six that evening Jane was laying the table for dinner at a house in Belsize Park. She was parlourmaid. Her friend, Amy, the kitchen-maid from Steeple End, had got her the job by " speaking " for her. Amy was cook.

In the kitchen they and the housemaid were a happy family of three. Jane was on her feet all day. From early morning to midnight the bell gave her scarcely fifteen minutes rest. The younger members of the Upstairs were a thoughtless and inconsiderate lot, and most of her life was spent on the staircase. But they were all very nice, and she was happy, and thought she had dropped into a good place. Set against the pawnshop it was an ideal place. She accepted a seventeen-hour day without knowing that it was a seventeen-hour day. She could not conceive life as meaning anything but hard work. Some people—gentry—had another kind of life, but they were people of different marrow and structure. There were not many of them. For people generally life meant hard work : it was as natural a law as breathing.

She lived in a cheerful shining kitchen, and the food was good. She had an afternoon off every week, and every other Sunday. Her morning print dress and her afternoon black dress were " found " by the house. She received fourteen pounds a year. Out of it she was saving again for the black silk dress.

The kitchen and the Upstairs lived on a basis of mutual and humorous friendship. On nights when dinner-parties meant extra work the master sent each of them a glass of sherry. He sent them a glass of sherry on their birthdays, and at Easter, and on the birthdays of members of the family. At Christmas they had glasses of champagne. He was a wine-merchant, and his calling lent him something of its own genial grace. He cracked jokes with all of them, and upon occasions he threw up gorgeous eruptions of ill-temper that were no more serious than his jokes. She remembered him with affection, and told tales of him years after he had forgotten that he ever had a parlourmaid named Cameron.

She was putting out the fish knives and forks when her mistress came to her. Mrs. Playne carried an open telegram. She spoke in tones that subtly smoothed the mistress attitude.

"Cameron, you must stop that. Hannah can finish it. You must get your hat and coat. You've been sent for."

"Sent for, m'm?" The phrase in domestic-servant circles had but one meaning. Her hands fumbled and she dropped a fish knife.

"Yes. Your father's had a—just—a—a slight accident."

"*Accident !*" The word shot into and back from her like a ball against a net.

"Now, now, my dear. Don't get worried, Cameron. He's had a fall. Nothing serious, I think, but they've had to take him to hospital. And they think you ought to know, and that you might like to go and see him. At St. Paul's Hospital. I should go now, if I were you. Don't wait for anything. And take a cab. Here's half a crown."

Of these words nothing went into her mind but "accident" and "hospital." Life became a cloud on which those two words glowed. In that cloud she blundered about and changed her frock and found hat and coat, and got into a cab.

The cab was one solid thing in a whirl of vapour. Out of the vapour came the beat of hoof and bell, and the yellow gush of shop windows, and the stab of lamps upon dark streets. They belonged to chaos and infinity. She knew

44

only cabs and hospitals. She did not conjecture what she would see at the hospital. She knew why she had been called, and her mind throbbed with fiendish repetition upon the thought of Saturday evenings and dripping-toast.

She entered the hospital without paying the driver. She was called out again by a violent "'Ere!" A minute later she did not know whether she had paid him or not, or how she had reached the hospital. Cabs had passed into the vapour.

They led her to the ward where Father lay. To reach the bed she had to pass round a screen. She did not see it or the bed. She saw only Father—not a tattered grey head and commonplace features, but a human face that was all human faces: the face that she had first fully seen in this world. In his presence she was aware that her whole being was a pain in the breast. She wanted to swoop upon him and comfort him and heal him. She wanted to fight incomprehensible death. She was a white patch of fury. She could have called death bad names. Her first words were—"Them cursed scaffolds!"

He brushed it aside. "That's all right, me gel. These things happen. Uncle Joe went like it. And Fred. It's all right. I'm comf'able now."

" Dadda ! "

" Glad you come so quick, gel. Don't know if they told you, but I ain't got long. And there's things I want to say. It's hard going like this— so sudden. No time to settle things. Still——"

" Dadda ! "

" Glad I was able to see you started. That's one comfort." The flush of life that had come to him with her entry was waning. He spoke sleepily. The words came in little gasps. " You're not a child now. That's one comfort. You're a young woman. And you got sense. I'm not worrying about you. You'll always remember what I taught you."

She wanted to say something quick and short that would convey to him the whole volume of her love and her remembrance of his goodness and her understanding of what he was trying to say. But all that would come was the repeated " Dadda ! "

His eyes answered her. " Keep yer end up. Pay yer way. And look everybody in the face. Always put a little bit by. Then you won't have to cringe to nobody. Won't have to ask charity. Keep away from that, whatever yeh do. 'Cos if you come to that, you come to th' end of every-thing. You might as well die then. You ain't a living creature then. You ain't got a soul.

46

Remember that song I used to sing you when you was little ? How'd it go ?

> " Always keep hold of a pound or two, boys,
>   In case there comes a day,
>   When the nimble shillings get too nimble
>   And dance right away."

" Don't, dadda ! "

" That was one of old Vance's. Yes. You was a little thing then. I could pick you up with one hand. You ain't much bigger now. Never mind. You was good when you was little. You always been good. You always will be good, won't you ? "

" Dadda ! "

" Remember that day I took you to Rosherville. And the steamer broke down ? And you'd eaten three bags of shrimps and got thirsty. And all the drink on the boat was finished ? Eh ? That was a good day. We've had some good days, ain't we ? That was a good day, too, at Steeple End. All the flowers—all the lovely flowers."

" You mustn't talk so much, dadda."

" It's all right, gel. Can't hurt me. And I got things to say. Yes. There'll be a pound or two left. Don't know whether the Works'll do anything for yeh. The insurance'll pay the expenses. Ah . . . here's Soph."

47

Aunt Sophy came round the screen. The angular face was flour-white. The eyes were hard; the lips tight. " Arthur ! "

" Soph ! "

For the sake of doing something Aunt smoothed the bed-clothes. They smiled at each other. Then he smiled at Jane, and Jane and Aunt smiled at each other. They all smiled. On this Jane discovered that she had been smiling all the time. She was shocked. She wondered how it was that she wasn't weeping, and how she could possibly smile. It seemed indecent. Her mind was settled upon the unfolding fact of Father's death. This little ant of thought bit her and distracted her from the fact. She found herself trying to work out the problem of why one smiled when one ought to weep. Everybody wept at these moments. But she didn't even feel sad; only a little sick.

He was dying. She knew that—she knew it fully, but she could not force the knowledge into her heart. There was nothing about him that suggested death. Certainly he looked dignified; more dignified than she thought he could look, and wholly at ease. Just as though it were Sunday morning, and he didn't want to get up. She could not reconcile this with dying. Dying was strange and awful; the only strange thing

48

about him was his dignity. He was dying, and as the spirit crept from the body it left with the perishing flesh something of its strength and integrity.

"You'll look after each other, won't you? You could take a lodger or two in the cottage, Soph, and keep things going that way. Jane's all right. She'll always be able to find a good place."

"Don't worry about us, Arthur. We shall be all right. We've got our health and strength. God will provide." And then, with a thrust of both hands to his face: "*Dear* brother!" Her bonnet shook with emotion. The beads on her cloak echoed it. Jane caught the echo.

This burst of sentiment from the harsh and acid Aunt Sophy did what the death-bed could not do. It shook her into conventional grief. She knelt by the bed and the tears dropped through her fingers. Father's eyes moved to her. They caressed her head. His hands were bandaged and immovable.

"You mustn't grieve, me gel. Grief's wicked. It's useless. Does nobody no good. Won't do me no good. Prayer does. Grief don't."

He appeared to sleep for a few seconds, and then to awake as though he had slept some hours. The voice was fainter and the words were halted.

"You're still—there, then." He wanted to say

E 49

something, and he struggled to say it. It seemed
to be of dire importance. It seemed that he
could not peacefully die until he had got it off his
mind. They bent over him as though this would
help. " What is it ? " After three quick breaths
he delivered it. " Is it—raining ? Looked like
—rain—just as—I—fell."

Aunt told him it was a fine evening. He said
" Ah," and seemed relieved to know it. He slept
again and woke again.

" You ain't much—like yer—mother, gel. But
you got her—strength. Nothing could—down
—her. She was a—good soul. You got to—
live on and—be a credit to me—and her. When
you—marry—remember—steadiness—important
thing. Love's no—good—without—that. Always do yer—job. Give yer—best. You'll be—
glad at—the end. You can—hold yer—head up."

He slept again and woke again. In a whisper
that carried barely an inch from his lips he said
" Pray."

They knelt and prayed. While they were praying he said sharply—" Oh ! " And again, but
in a higher key, " Oh ! " And then a long
" O-oh." And then he said, looking straight
before him, " Oh—beautiful. Beautiful. Beautiful." They rose from their knees. On the third
" beautiful " something gave him the power to

spread out his splinted arms to greet the beautiful. Then he dropped them, and fell back, and was still.

Jane thought she would never be happy again.

6.

UNDER the nervous twilight of a March evening Charing Cross was in tumult. On the massed crowds rain dropped in a million lances. With raised umbrellas and blank faces the people pressed through these lances like a Chinese army. As the lances fell before the shop-lights they were split into needles of gold and silver. The sky was a stew of clouds that took no shapes, yet hinted always at shapes beyond the knowledge or retention of the human eye. They had not the harsh hue of brutality, but the delicate chill of cruelty. It was a sky that drove men's minds gratefully towards the common-sense of buses and greasy pavements.

Off these greasy pavements and out of the leaden air Jane stepped timidly into a world of light and colour. Great glass doors, padded with felt, opened to receive her. When they closed upon her it was as though she had gone deaf. No harsh breath of the bickering streets came to this world; nothing of the ungainly business of living.

With the brown mud still upon her shoes she stood in the vast hall of a temple consecrated to an unknown god. Its builders had ransacked the arts of all the continents and the achievements of all the ages. She walked ankle-deep in velvet. Pillars of black marble streamed up the walls to lose themselves in a rose-window in the roof. Bowls of alabaster threw the light of their lamps against the marble, which diffused it into soft pools of yellow. A Titanic staircase of agate and brass made flamboyance round the iron filigree of the lift-cage. A fire of logs and coal blazed in a copper cradle. Glossy corridors led to silk-curtained doors, and these led madly to other corridors. From some secret chapel of the temple came the discreet music of an orchestra—silver swathed in silk.

In its towering immensity it seemed to be a temple dreamed by some wrathful king of the Koran, some striding shaker of the world from the golden rocks of Asia.

Crushed by this magnificence, Jane went humbly to a desk marked " Inquiries " and presented her letter of recommendation.

A week later she was working on one of the terraces of this terraced temple. She was chambermaid at London's first big hotel.

She began to see the life of another world than

the world of comfortable houses, and the first sight of it shocked her. She was familiar with ladies and gentlemen, and their ways, and she was familiar with dining-rooms and drawing-rooms. But although she was still among ladies and gentlemen, they presented unsuspected phases. She had seen them in their homes, and as guests in other homes, and had thought that they were thus and thus. Her experience at the hotel challenged her ideas, and worried her. She decided that hotel manners were due to new-fangled ways. She didn't like new-fangled ways. They upset everything.

The ladies who stayed in the hotel were demonstrably ladies, but there were things about some of them that compelled her to hold back the loving respect she had given to Lady Mellonspar and Mrs. Playne and her last mistress. The highest wages could not have tempted her to take a private engagement with some of them. They had all the qualities that she looked for in ladies. Their manners were easy and assured, and they were gracious to her, and kind; kinder than most ladies. But she whispered to Aunt Sophy a well-founded suspicion that some of them were—well—kept. It was a dreadful word, and she could only whisper it, and nod. She had no definite proof, but she was as sure as sure.

She had thought that only common women were like that. But these were regal. Counts and Princes called on them. That made it the greater pity. She was thirty-nine. She knew enough about life to understand their situation, and had enough prejudice to be appalled by it. It was only because they were still ladies that she did not give up her position. It was a very good position.

The work was hard, but she was used to that; and the money was " good." She was not used to that. The ladies were lavish in their recognition of service; just a little more lavish than serious ladies should have been. She had not been there three months before a City draper delivered the black silk dress.

For twenty years she had been looking towards that dress, and at last it was achieved. She felt as the artist feels at the consummation of a work that has long eluded him. It brought none of the thrill that it would have brought had she achieved it in the first flush of desire for it; she was just quietly satisfied. Her original purpose in achieving it had been the display of it to Father as proof of industry. It had now no purpose : it was merely something done. But life gave her the consolation prize that it gives to all its small folk. There was a Sunday afternoon when she went to see Amy at her new place at Kensington Gore. The silk dress was recognised and acclaimed.

"*Jane!* How sweetly pretty, to be sure. Why, you'd pass *any*where for a lady."

The dress was considered against the exacting standard of all silk dresses. It became the silk dress of the minute. Defeated of its original purpose, it yet did something for her. It ranked and ranged her. Thereafter it was known that hers was a black silk mind. It demanded of life the quietly good.

It was in the black silk mood that love and marriage came to Jane. It came without fire and without shock.

On her terrace of the ten terraces was a floor-waiter of gentle and agreeable ways. Amid their duties they met constantly in the corridor, and he began to be alertly and markedly respectful. He was abrupt or facetious with the other chamber-maid of that floor: he had no levity for Jane. He performed small services without any air of performing them. His attitude was a gallant kindness, and he did not elaborate it. There was no nonsense about him. This made Jane consider him. He had pale blue eyes and a sharp moustache. He was no longer young, but he was the speediest waiter on that floor. Nobody

56

seemed to notice it. He wasn't popular with the guests; his manner held a touch of independence.

One afternoon she was waiting in the Strand for a bus to Clerkenwell. While she was waiting, he passed. They had not met outside the hotel. He lifted his hat and bowed. He asked, with a smile, if he might stop the bus for her and see her in. She thanked him. He said it would be a pleasure. In a few moments of chat, he wondered whether she would like to see the decorations in the West End for the coming Royal Visit. He had been told that they were very good. Perhaps, on the next afternoon when they were both off. . . . She thanked him and thought it would be very nice.

A fortnight later they walked some two miles round the West End admiring the fairy lamps and the bunting. During the walk they found that their attitudes to life were those of twins. On every topic that arose their opinions were common. Towards the end of the walk he thought she must be tiring, and deferentially offered his arm. She took it, and they talked more freely. They discovered mutual dislike of the go-ahead times, and the foolish race, on the part of the young, for pleasure. Neither could see what the young meant by it. He listened closely to her views, and remarked how refreshing it was to meet a young woman who really *thought*. There were very few of them about. Flightiness seemed to be The Thing to-day. He deprecated flightiness. She thought it disgusting. He said that most young women thought him a dry old stick. Perhaps he was. He wasn't up to their flighty ways. That was why he had never married. All the girls he had met seemed to think of nothing but gadding about. He didn't think that made for a happy married life, and so had never married. She thought he had been very sensible.

At the end of the walk he asked whether he might offer her a little refreshment, and indicated one of the new tea-shops. They went in and ordered coffee and biscuits. At a quiet table in a corner they related personal history by anecdote, and discovered how similar their lives had been.

To receive attention and deference was a new sensation for Jane. It warmed her. She did not allow it to thrill her : within her wall of prudence thrills were suspect.

He escorted her back to the hotel. To avoid foolish and offensive talk they agreed that he should enter ten minutes after her. Before they parted they fixed another outing for the nearest afternoon when their off-times coincided.

In Jane's mind that year was Regent's Park, and Regent's Park was a span of life with glowing edges. Trust and affection were the light that threw the glow. Their favourite spot was the northern point of the lake. They sat there so often during the year that every detail of the scene was registered upon the plate of her mind. Twenty-five years later she could evoke it and live in it.

They were sitting there one afternoon under September bronze. It was the seventh month of their walking out. In the middle of amiable talk Robert said : " I saw some very nice rooms in Whitcomb Street last night."

" Did you ? "

" Yes. Very nice rooms. Nice respectable street, too. And near the hotel. Would you—would you like to look at them one afternoon ? "

" Yes, I think I would."

That was the first expression they had given to the drift of their friendship. With those remarks he had proposed and she had accepted. Everything was then understood. They allowed the hotel staff to congratulate them.

He never spoke of love, nor did she; but all their talk was warm and rich. To this warmth the flower of life responded and slowly opened. They talked of bargains in carpets and easy-chairs and curtains. Of the money she could save by making some of the fittings herself. Of whether they could keep a cat in lodgings. Of how she would manage to cook on an old-fashioned fire-place. Of a new hotel that was being opened, and his chances of bettering himself. Of how foolish it was to try to be economical by buying cheap meat.

The next few weeks were weeks of zest. They went round the second-hand shops, sometimes singly, sometimes together. They had victories and defeats. They were building a home in a world that didn't want them to build a home. It made them fight for it. When they snatched a trophy of bedstead or chair or tea-set, they hurried to tell each other.

Within two months they had achieved the solid necessaries. The rest, they agreed, it would be sensible to get little by little. They settled down in Whitcomb Street, and Jane possessed her first home and was proud of it. It was to be her apex of achievement. Robert approved her arrangement of it. In one burst of sentiment he called her his Little Wonder and kissed her. She laughed and went on with her dusting.

She had some comfortable chairs and a plush hearth-rug. The walls held a coloured print of Millais' Red Riding Hood, a steel engraving of the Trial of Earl Russell and a panorama of Brighton from the sea. The floor-staff of the hotel gave them a dinner service, and other aids to the home came from Amy and Nurse and Aunt Sophy.

Life flowed through a passage of quiet beauty. She was not aware of its beauty then. She was so busy living it. Later she saw it and knew that it had been too beautiful.

In Robert's free hours they had rides on the tram, and trips to the Crystal Palace, and now and then a theatre. The free hours of the winter he spent in his special easy-chair, smoking and telling stories of the hotels he had worked at. He was a mimic, and he brought some of the world's great ones to ridiculous life. She listened in purring bliss.

His hours were irregular, but she was always ready for him. The fireplace was small, but the chimney " drew " well. With a little contrivance she was able to provide excellent meals. Her life was centred on providing excellent meals. She brought to the business of these meals the hard heat of coke. Had the world interfered with the preparing of Robert's meals she would have fought the world. The world would have retired.

7.

A MAN was standing in a public-house in a byway of Piccadilly. He was telling his friend certain pungent truths of life which the fret of living had thrown up to his sensitive eye.

They stood in a room which looked as though it had started to be the smoking-room of a West End club, and then had gone mad. It offered the parable of the sensible man suddenly denying the key of his life and losing himself in discord.

There were deep chairs of brown hide, large lounges of brown hide; mahogany tables; Turkey carpet; mosaic paving; stone fireplace. The ceiling reproduced the flowered carving of the ceiling of a baronial hall. The baronial note was abruptly challenged by the walls. Two of them were covered by giant mirrors. The surfaces of the mirrors carried flaming gilt scrolls of the Royal Arms and the insignia of a great brewery. A legend in red lettering said that the beer of this brewery was supplied to great personages by (yellow lettering) Royal Appointment. A large card in harsh reds and blues showed a soldier

walking with a prostitute. It announced somebody's lemonade. It hung on a wall that was
oak-panelled. On other panels were crude draw-
ings representing some characters of Dickens;
coloured posters of fat men in green drinking
amber whisky; half-naked girls in furious pink
and white drinking lime-juice; and a picture of
a short-kilted and red-nosed Highlander lying
drunk in the heather. A large diploma in a gilt
frame stated in faulty grammar that the landlord
of the house was a member of the Bazooka's
Club. A poster on yellow paper, hanging over
the mouth of the Saxon fireplace, stated that
somebody's stout was good for nursing mothers.
On the Turkey carpet, just below the counter,
was a range of ugly spittoons. The carpet around
them showed that their ugly presence was unjusti-
fied.

The man was like the room. He had reached
the male climacteric and was swerving from his
intent.

"Tell you what it is. I've had about enough
of it. Day after day, day after day. Always the
same. No change. No excitement. What's it
for? Eh? Slave, slave, slave. Same grind every
day. And what d'you get out of it at the end?
Here am I—at my age—and what have I had out
of it? Nothing. And so we go on."

His friend tilted his bowler to the affable angle. " Well, what else is there to do ? "

" *What else ?* " The tone held down-glancing scorn. " Nothing, I s'pose, for them that don't think. But to a *thinking* man it's—it's deplorable. Deplorable. Here am I, when I ought to be retiring—after a life of slave, slave, slave—and what chance have I got ? None. Just got to go on. You slave and slave. You think you'd like to settle down. You find the right woman and marry. And then after a bit it goes on just as dull as before. And then you die. And what've you got outa life ? Nothing."

The friend was philosophic. " Well, what d'y' expect ? That's life, me boy."

" Oh, no, it isn't Oh, no. Look at the lives some people have. Look at the people in my place. The Majestic. *They* get something outa life. And why d'they get it ? Eh ? Why ? "

" Well, they—I s'pose they got it to begin with, or they work for it."

" Oh, no. Oh, no. Least, on'y a few of 'em. They get it because they take it. That's how they get it. They take it. They don't slave, slave, slave. They don't get married and have a kid, and then have to slave again. They take their fun whenever they want it."

" Well, what you get married for ? "

64

"Eh? Oh . . . I dunno. Well, at my age a man wants a place of his own."

"Well, you got a place of yer own. What more d'yeh want? Can't have everything."

He appeared to turn this over in his mind as though it were a rebus. He decided that it wasn't, and jumped some paces ahead of the talk. "Women are rum."

"Ah."

"I dunno what marriage does, but it seems to change people. Changes both of 'em. After marriage somehow you don't seem to like what you useta like."

"That's right. You're quite right there. It —it changes you."

"That's it. You alter. I always thought that a nice quiet sensible woman was just the woman I could be happy with. But . . . I dunno. I'm not so sure now. I always was a quiet one, as you know. Naturally quiet. But it seems now that I've sorta missed something. I haven't had my fun. I feel now that a girl with a bit of Go . . ." He raised his voice. "Like Bella here. Eh, Bella?"

Bella turned. She was serving a customer in another bar. She became arch. "None of your nonsense now, Mr. Wilson."

"That's all right, Bella." He illuminated things

to his friend. "Bella and me understand one another. There's a go-er for you. Quite steady, mind, but bright. Bright. Pays for dressing. Stylish."

The friend considered him. He tilted his bowler to the back of his head. "Seems to me, ole man, you're bored. You want a change."

"As a matter o' fact, ole man, between you and I, that's just what I do want. I'm sick of everything. I haven't had my fun."

The friend nodded. "Ah. 'M. Often happens with quiet fellers when they get on in years. Seen it happen. You woke up too late. But speaking as a pal, ole man, don't have the change with Bella. I know her better'n you. Unless, of course, you *like* wild cats. She'll have all the fur off you. Look what she done to young Mason. Cleaned him right out."

"That's all right, ole man. I lived long enough to be able to take care of meself. And I dessay young Mason got something for his trouble. I been sensible too long. There was a lady at a hotel I worked at once. In Albemarle Street. I could have had the time of my life. But I was a fool. I didn't take it when I could. People who want things take 'em. Nobody'll give 'em to you. Them that get the best outa life are the Takers. I been a fool. You'll have one more?

66

. . . Yes, do. Bella—my gentleman friend and me desire some nourishment. . . . That's the style. How nicely you pour it out. Right in the glass every time. Couldn't do it better meself. And I've filled a few in my time. Mostly for other people—more fool me."

"You *are* chatty to-day, Mr. Wilson. But there—I like people to be bright and chatty. After all, what's the good of being miserable? You only live once. Might just as well be bright and chatty." She patted her padded coiffure. She gave them the limited smile of a woman accustomed to receiving flattering attention.

" That's what I always say."

" Yes, that's the idea."

" Yes. You want a bit o'life when you have to work hard, don't you? Like you and me. Speaking of work, what you doing on your Wednesday afternoon? "

The friend frowned. Bella polished a glass severely. " Now then, go on with you, Mr. Wilson. You and your Wednesday afternoons! "

" No, but really. . . ." He leaned across the bar. " How you fixed for Wednesday? What about a little bite of dinner and a theatre, eh? "

The friend sighed, and set his bowler hat at a business angle. He considered that he had done his best to save old Bob Wilson.

Wednesday night was one of Robert's early nights. He was off at seven and home by half-past. That Wednesday night he wasn't home, and the supper was spoiled. He wasn't home by eight, or nine, or ten. He was home at half-past eleven.

Jane greeted him brightly. " Here you are, then. But I'm afraid it won't be very nice. I been keeping it hot. Didn't your relief turn up ? Did you have to stay on ? "

But he was short in his manner. " Eh ? Yes, I was kept. Yes."

" I'll just make it nice and hot, and——"

" Oh, I shan't want 'ny supper."

" Don't want 'ny *supper?* After you been on all these hours ? "

" What ? No. I had a bite in the pantry."

From the bedroom came a wail. She was busy with a saucepan. He sat down and stared at the fire. The wail increased. He jerked a hand outward. " Oh, for goodness' sake, stop the kid's howling. When a man comes home tired. This squalling."

The tone was so out of his key that she almost dropped the saucepan. It might have been a stranger sitting there. Never in their two years of married life had he spoken like this. Never had he called Baby " the kid." She put the saucepan down and looked at him with concern. She was careful that he should not know she was looking. He must be ill. Perhaps one of the gentlemen had given him some drink and played a trick with it. That had happened to other waiters in the hotel. She was sorry for him. She hesitated between comforting him and soothing the baby, and couldn't start one for thought of the other. He made the decision for her. " Oh, go on—go on."

She went into the bedroom and tried to hush the child. She hung some coats and skirts over the door. She hoped that this would hold the sound from the other room. She decided that she mustn't ask him any questions. Men didn't like questions when they were upset. She'd just take no notice and treat him as his usual self. When the child was on the way to sleep she came out and cleared the table. She told him that Mrs. Glass, downstairs, had lost her dog. He grunted. She told him that the greengrocer across the way was shutting up and going to settle with his married son in Canada. He grunted. She went softly about the business of putting the room in order for to-morrow. After some minutes she suggested that if he was tired he'd probably like to go to bed.

" What's the good o' going to bed? How

can one sleep in there—with the kid waking up and howling ? ''

She was now certain that he was ill. She said she would make him up a bed in the living-room. She went into the bedroom, and came out wrestling with cushions and blankets and a sheet. The world was in uproar about her ears, and it was put upon her to calm it. Blankets and cushions were all the weapons she had. With these she faced it. Out of that cloud of weapons peered a dishevelled figure and a straight mouth.

She made up a bed on the sofa. It was a second-hand bargain : a new kind of sofa with a movable head which went flat with the seat. She worked at the bed with quiet fury. She patted it, and re-made parts of it, and patted it again. She told him she was sure it would be comfortable. She urged him to get into it and have a good night's rest. He grunted. She waited a moment, wondering whether she should kiss him good-night. She had not handled this situation before. She decided that she'd better not. She said " Good-night, dear." He gave a growl with the word " night " in it. She went into the bedroom.

She got up early, so that she could give him a nice cup of tea. If he'd been made ill by some wrong kind of drink, a cup of tea in the morning would be necessary. She went into the living-room to light the fire. She went in with stealth for fear of awaking him before the tea was ready.

He wasn't there.

The bed made with such care sprawled before her just as she had left it. Its white pillow and sheet showed her a face of contempt. It appeared to know that it had been created for nothing, and it jeered its creator.

She saw a piece of paper on the mantelpiece. It was fixed under a vase showing a view of Margate. They had bought the vase on a day trip. She took it down carefully. It was a letter. Before she read it she put the view of Margate back into its place.

" I am very sorry Jane but I find I made a mistake. I am sick of everything and I am going off. It isn't your fault it is me. I ought not to have married at all. I am not that sort. You were so nice you got on my nerves that was the trouble. I am going out of the country so it is no good trying to find me. I am a bad lot and you won't be bothered by me any more. You deserve someone better than me.

" ROBERT."

That was all. She read it, and then looked about the room, as though expecting to see him hiding in some corner. She felt the paper to be sure that it was real paper. She tried to think.

71

How could an angel become a devil in a few days? He must have gone off his head. People didn't change like that. She was sure she had never been deceived in him. He wasn't that sort when she married him : nothing like that sort. He must have had a sudden attack of something. She wanted to run after him and tend him. It wasn't *like* him. But she read the letter again, and the voice, in its undertones, was the voice of Robert. She had heard those tones in his talk when things went wrong at the hotel. He had changed—that was all. She remembered here certain little signs of irritation, forerunners of this letter. He had changed. He hadn't been bad. He had gone bad. She had always believed that people were bad and bad, or good and good, as God made them. The truth that she now dimly perceived unloosed the fixed stars of her heaven, and they reeled about her.

She dropped the letter and stumbled into the bedroom. She fell on her knees and gathered her baby in her arms and pressed its face against hers. She sobbed and wept in great hacking coughs. Formless words came out of the coughs.

Then, against her tense grip, the baby cried, and she got up and soothed it, and set about lighting the fire and making the bed.

She never saw Robert again.

8.

At forty-five Jane was scrubbing the vestibule of a West End theatre. She received one-and-sixpence for a morning's work. She sent the flannel across the floor with an expression of assault. She scrubbed with a fury that battling soldiers never know. As she scrubbed she sang a popular song with words of La, la, la.

The rooms in Whitcomb Street were gone. The black silk dress and the wedding dress were gone. Most of the furniture was gone. She had a bed and a table and two chairs; some cups and saucepans and a tea-pot. She had her daughter Agatha. She was happy.

She had one room in Berwick Street that was wholly hers. It cost three shillings a week, and she could pay three shillings a week. To supplement her morning work she had work on three afternoons at a shilling the afternoon. With twelve regular shillings a week she could look the world in the face.

But sometimes, in the evenings, when Agatha was in bed, and she sat lonely in her home, she was afraid. She had nothing to do, and the silence and the solitude bred spectres. She could not have the friendly rustle of a fire : only on Sundays did she dare its cost. She could not read because papers meant pennies, and often she sat in the dark because candles meant pennies. And on the dark were painted fingers that threatened to tear her home from her. To be out of work was to be at the mercy of those fingers. All within that tiny cube was hers, but she knew that to hold it she must keep everlasting vigil. The world envied her that home, and if she wavered the fingers would grab it. Each night she prayed for more work and thanked God for the work she had. She was not religious, but she felt it right to believe in God, and did. Regularly at night she thanked Him for letting the day pass without disaster to her and her child. She asked Him to bless those good people who gave her lots of scrubbing. She did not ask for spiritual grace, or for strength to keep His commandments, or for forgiveness of her sins. She asked only that she might never be out of work.

From being out of work the downward path was easy. It led to debt and workhouse. To be touched by these things was to be put outside the world of wholesome creatures. Unclean ! Unclean ! Between death and this contact many folk of Rudy's Court had chosen death. These had been held to be noble. Those who had the bailiff in had been spoken of in awed mutters. Murderers were only hanged. These others were seen as creatures marked for the scourge of God. People did not like to be caught speaking to them. Fear of this fate was the basis of all her praying.

Every few weeks her only friend, Amy, came to see her. At each visit she brought something to help the battle. A packet of candles. A quarter-pound of tea. A knitted vest for Agatha. A piece of steak. Sometimes, after one of her visits, Jane would find a two-shilling-piece on the mantelshelf. On these occasions she did not hold her prayers till bedtime. She knelt straight down at the table and offered an interim prayer for blessings upon Amy, and thanks that her humble self should be blessed with such a friend.

For fourpence a week the old woman in the next room " minded " Agatha while she was at work. It was another blessing that God had made Agatha a good girl. She was five, but she had no views on a five-year-old's rights. She was happy with her mother or with strangers. She ate contentedly whatever there was to eat. Jane was firm with her and allowed no nonsense. She did not believe in petting children, and she had no endearing names for her. She was concerned with bringing her up "nicely." Agatha rewarded her concern. The supreme tribute came from the old woman in the next room. "Such a dear little girl. You couldn't tell but what she wasn't a lady's child. How you keep her so nice, I don't know."

The old woman had a right to speak. She had worked for real ladies. To all the new lodgers she related anecdotes of these ladies. The tone of these anecdotes conveyed that she had been friends with the Archangel Gabriel. Sometimes at night she asked Jane to join her in a little drop of something. She was very fond of a little drop of something, and Jane knew its value at moments of utter exhaustion. But she was afraid. It might start a habit. It was all very well for the old woman, who had a pension, but Jane had her living to earn. A moment's withdrawal of attention and it might be gone.

Life was recovering from Robert, and things were going well. She had been left alone and penniless, and in her search for work had been handicapped by the child. But she had come through. She was living respectably. If at the end of her life she could say " I always kept myself respectable," she would die as happily as the saints. But she knew that she was living only by the grace of others. Once that grace—the giving of work—was withdrawn, she must sink. It was her nightly haunting. The time came when it took substance.

Her fellow-cleaner in the theatre came to her one morning with news.

"You know that sergeant—at the stage-door? He's a mean one, if you like. Goodness knows what he makes in tips, but whatever he makes—never satisfied. Grab, grab, grab. Got three children, all out earning, and now he's trying to get work for his wife. Heard him ask for it. What a family! Can't understand people of that sort. Here's other people need work, so's to live, and here's them that don't need it running after it and taking it away from them that do. I heard him asking the manager if he could work her in. Heard him telling him what a good worker she was. I lay he'll get someone out and work her in. Blast him. He's that crafty and underhand he'd do anything. We shall have to look out, else——"

Something clammy caught hold of Jane's breast. "You think——"

"Ah. . . . We shall have to look out."

All that week Jane worked in fear. Her eyes and ears were detectives, seeking hints and clues

77

of impending changes. She worked with greater zest than her ill-nourished body could support. She wanted to show that no sergeant's wife could work so swiftly or so well. She made her scrubbing a spectacle. Nobody attended it. She made herself ill. By the middle of the next week she could scarcely scrub. This was noticed. She was asked if she was ill. She asserted that she wasn't. She was told that she had better go home. She was certain that she need not go home; she could get on all right. There was nothing the matter with her. She was told that half the morning was gone, and she'd only done a quarter of the work. She said that she was a little tired, that was all. She had harsh words for liars, but she lied. She said she'd been up all night with her baby. They said they were sorry about that, but after all a theatre was a serious thing. Its workers must be fit.

Her hands snatched at the last few wisps of vigour that her pulse held. The scrubbing-brush became insane.

Next day she got up, and, in the middle of dressing, fell down. She could not go to the theatre. Even the need of the one-and-sixpence and the fear of the sergeant's wife would not inspire her slack limbs. She had no afternoon work that day, and she spent it in bed. She got

up only to get Agatha's meals—bread and milk
and a banana for dinner, and bread and treacle
for supper. She could eat nothing herself, and
was thankful: there was very little to eat. At
night she drank a cup of condensed milk mixed
with cold water, and was able to sleep.

In the morning she was tottery, but she got up
and plodded to the theatre. She was met in the
vestibule by the commissionaire. He told her
that his orders were that she need not come again.
They had had to fill the place with a stronger
woman. He was sorry.

She had expected this, but the impact of it
rocked her. She moved from foot to foot, and
looked up at the giant's face. She appeared to be
waiting for an answer to a question. He repeated
that he was sorry, but those were the orders, and
went invitingly to the door. She waited in the
middle of the vestibule. She looked bleakly
about her as though parting from a beloved
home. He came back to her, and said, "Well,
that's what they told me." She looked at the
floor. "Yes, the place was filled yesterday.
Sorry." She looked at the box office. It was
early morning, and his professional geniality was
not in full flow. "Don't you understand?"

"Eh? Oh, yes. Yes—of course I understand. I'm not wanted any more. I see."

" Well, then——"

At last she went. Even then she looked back.
She was like a condemned murderer who will not
until eight o'clock abandon thought of a reprieve.
She stood for some seconds on the pavement,
unable to go firmly away, lest some sudden change
of mind should happen in the high quarters
beyond the doors. Then, slowly, so that she
might still be overtaken, she crept home.

She looked at the bed and longed to drop into
it. But she knew that she must not. She must
go out and look for work. There was one spot
of solace. She had her afternoon job. The
three shillings that she got for those three afternoons covered the rent. Food one could do
without—at least, she thought so. Clothes could
be made to serve. Her elemental need was a
roof over her head. So long as she had some
corner of her own in which to sleep she could
carry on; and the first purpose of all her being
was to have the rent ready. The rent. The
rent. She went downstairs walking to its beat,
and thanking God for the afternoon job.

She walked from street to street, looking for
registry offices and those shops that showed cards
in their windows announcing " places." She did
not know where these were to be found. She
could only walk at random through street after

Street, peering from side to side for any sign of them. She found three. None of them had any places that she could fill. She was no longer smart enough for hotel work, and Agatha barred her from any chance of a regular indoor position. But her neat appearance impressed the people, and they took her name and particulars of the work she could do. At one shop the girl expressed surprise that she should be seeking cleaner's work —her manner was so much above it. She explained her circumstances and got a little tinge of pleasure from the mournful tour by showing her " characters " from Lady Mellonspar and Mrs. Plane and the Majestic Hotel. The girl said she had never seen such letters. People ought to jump at her. She promised to do her best for her.

After wondering whether it would be wiser to try other shops, or to rest, she decided that it would be wiser to rest. She went home. She wrote to Amy and told her of the disaster. She asked her, if she heard of anything, to " speak " for her. At three o'clock in the afternoon she went to bed.

On rent day she had three shillings and seven-pence. She paid over the three shillings, and tried to plan the sevenpence to its supreme significance. Life's anodyne, her cup of tea, must go. The Sunday fire and light must go. She had a small spirit-lamp and enough methylated spirit to allow her to boil something. She bought a tin of milk at twopence-halfpenny, a pennyworth of stale bread, and two-pennyworth of butcher's bones. This would serve them until Monday, and still leave her three-halfpence.

She was aware of complete exhaustion and futility. She stewed the bones and gave Agatha for dinner a cupful of the liquor with the bread soaked in it. She sat to the table with Agatha and ate a piece of bread and sucked one of the bones. She looked at the meal and she looked at her home, and thought of Monday. Great tears began to roll down her cheeks. Agatha noted the tears with concern, and found a cause for them. She offered her cup. " Have some o' this, Mummy. It's nicer'n the bone."

She pushed the cup away, and sobbed. Agatha considered the puzzle of her mother, and went on eating.

Each day of the next week she spent in looking for work, and found none. Nobody but Amy knew of her trouble, but at the end of the week she was forced to speak of it at the place where she worked the three afternoons. They gave her some scraps from the kitchen. She spread these over four days.

On Tuesday she had a note from Amy, telling

her that a friend of Amy's who had a friend who worked at a house in Tufnell Park had told her that they wanted a daily woman. She set out that morning and walked the four miles to Tufnell Park. Her three-halfpence had gone in bread.

When she reached the house she was hot and weak. The woman of the house looked troubled. "Dear-dear! Now if you'd only come yesterday I think you'd have just suited us. But we made arrangements yesterday with a woman the milkman recommended. I *am* sorry. Such a long way to come, too."

As she went out through the bushy front garden her eye noted a glitter. Under a laurel-bush, screened from the house by a holly tree, lay some coins. She went to the bush, and saw that the coins had scattered from an open purse. They made about eight shillings. She picked up those on the ground and put them with the others in the grey purse. She went back to the house and rang. She asked the maid who answered the door if anybody in the house had lost a purse. The maid said that Miss Evelyn lost her grey purse last night. Miss Evelyn was that careless. The maid thanked her for bringing it in.

She walked back to Soho. She called at the three registry offices, but they had nothing for her. She went home and looked about her room for something to sell. She had no views against selling things. There was planetary distance between selling and pawning. The highest people sold their pictures and their jewels. Pawning was only for the lowest poor—for drunkards and draggle-tails. But she could see nothing that would sell. While she was ransacking the box that held her few precious trifles, the old woman in the next room came to her.

"Agatha was crying while I was minding her. She said she was hungry."

Jane met her eyes like one caught in sin. She groped for something to say that would deny the truth of the hunger. The old woman gave her no chance to find it. "Now look here, me dear, I know you've lost your work, and that you haven't got much behind you. Mrs. Joyce heard from the theatre that they'd put someone else in, and she told Mrs. Doon downstairs. And I know you must be having a hard time. Now I got a few shillings in the Post Office, and I know you're an honest body. Now let me lend you a bit till things get better. I can't bear a child being hungry."

Jane waved an agitated hand, as though repulsing dirt. "No. Oh, no. Thank you all the same, but I never borrowed yet. And never will.

It's very kind of you. Very kind. But no. I couldn't. I couldn't. Once get into debt. . . ."

" I think you're very silly, me dear. It isn't everybody I'd offer it to. Very few, come to that. It's only because you——"

" I know, I know." The tone was as agitated as the hand. It seemed to doubt its own strength of refusal. " But I couldn't, I couldn't."

" But the child——"

" I'll find some way, I'll find some way. I've always held my head up. I've never been beholden. It's good of you, but——"

" Oh, well, if you feel like that, me dear. But if you can't get anything, and the child's hungry, why don't you go on the parish? You got a better right than most of 'em."

The agitated tone burst into flame. " *Parish !* " She flung back the word as a virtuous woman might fling back the word whore. " Parish ! Me? *Charity !* " The old woman flinched before the spark of the voice. She scratched her head and went away wondering where she had offended.

Jane sat on the bed and stared at the wall. She had not guessed that the house knew they were starving. It was the crushing load on her load of trouble. She could hear them whispering to each other—" I don't believe that child gets enough to eat." She tortured herself with a

85

mental echo of their whispers and a vision of their scandalised faces. Privacy was her passion. Always she had wanted to live behind her walls unseen and untalked-of. And now she was being talked-of and pitied. She wanted to get up in that minute and flee from the house.

But she couldn't. She could only sit and stare. Agatha hungry. People talking. The parish. Her mind wandered from these things and her vision was blurred. She saw a coloured balloon floating about the room, and remembered that she had once been happy. She wondered whether she would ever be able to get coloured balloons for Agatha. Soon the room was whirling with coloured balloons and parishes.

When it ceased whirling she learnt from a church chime that she had been sitting on the bed for three hours. The whirling had done her good. She felt much stronger. She wasn't the sort that went on the parish. She couldn't go on the parish. Something would happen to stop that. Work *must* come along in a day or two.

It didn't. The scraps from the afternoon-place were casual, and Agatha was still hungry. To get food she broke into the shillings that covered the rent. On Saturday she had only one-and-threepence.

That morning a visitor called. The landlord

knocked at her door. Mr. Doon had the in-
definite hue of the spider, and although not ill
he crawled. His web was in the basement, and
he seldom came out of it. In all the time she
had been there she had only once seen him. He
looked as though he had never at any time really
dressed himself, and would not know how to
begin. The clothes he wore hung about him,
and always something—socks or collar or braces
—was missing. He was small and lean-faced,
with a sudden stomach. The face wore straggles
of hair that were neither beard nor moustache.
He breathed audibly. His smile, if one did not
examine it, was pleasant. His movements were
soft.

He addressed her with surprise, as though he
had come upon her in the street. His voice was
husky. "Hul-lo, Mrs. Wilson. Well. . . . Yes.
I just called up. I heard you was having a bit of
trouble, and I thought to meself. . . . So I just
called up. Yes. I thought perhaps I might be
of some help. Yes. I don't like to hear of a
respectable little woman like you being in trouble.
When there's those that could help them. No."

He paused, to give opportunity to his smile.
He held it for some seconds, working it upon
her, as flint upon steel. It failed to strike from
her any responsive glance. She looked at him,

waiting to hear his business. He seemed ill at ease.

"No. When there's those that could help them. Not likely. I mean to say, when you want a friend. . . . There's times when we all want a friend, eh? I thought if we had a little talk about it. You can trust *me*. I know where respect's due, and I give it. When I see a widow all alone in the world, doing her best, I feel—I feel—what I mean, it's sad. A woman wants someone to look after her."

He smiled. Jane's mind was not present. It was settled upon the one fact that she could not pay the rent. The attitude of those to whom the rent was due did not interest her. She said "Yes," without knowing what she was expressing accord with.

"Now what I felt was—here's this respectable little lady, all alone. And she's in trouble. And here am I. I mean—there's you and there's me. I'm not as hard as I look, reely. One has to be hard with some o' the people I've had here. They'd do you in no time if you wasn't. But I'm not reely hard. I'm reely as soft as the next man. And I'm not old, either. I'm not likely to be hard on you. I just wanted to let you know. Not"—he waved a hand and swung his head, as though annihilating the idea—"likely.

Don't you worry. If you need a friend—
well. . . ."

He smiled. He peered through the doorway
and down the stairs, and listened. He turned
again to the room. Jane was standing by the
table, still waiting for him to state his business.
The silence ceased to be a may-fly pause in talk.
It grew into something sentient and significant.
He moved a step farther into the room, and
rubbed his hands. The silence began to tingle
on his ears. He looked through the window and
addressed the street.

"I mean to say, when two people know their
way about the world, and it's a case of trouble.
. . . I wish you'd let me help you." He looked
straight at her, without smiling. His pale eyes
held a watery warmth. "Let me send you up
some dinner. Eh? And after that we could
have a talk about the trouble. Eh?"

When he came farther into the room she was
startled into clear attention. She listened to his
words and watched him. As she met his downward glance on the offer of dinner, she understood his reference to people who knew their
way about the world. The understanding brought
her fully awake, and her face came alight and
warm. He mistook this light for something that
it wasn't. He moved a step nearer to her, and

89

his arm left his side. At the first movement of
the arm Jane stepped back and reached for something. Her hand found the handle of an enamel
saucepan. She aimed it. A voice tore out of
her throat like the voice of a furious parrot.

"Out of my room—you! Out of my room!
Out! Out! Quick! Out!"

Each word was a stab. He fell back, shocked
and indignant. The parts of his face that were
not covered with hair showed white. His eyes
took alarm. "Quiet, woman. Quiet, you fool.
Sh!" He waved a hand towards the stairs.

"Out, then! Out! Or——"

He shot through the door. She slammed it
upon him and locked it.

Ten minutes later she found herself still facing
the door and still holding the enamel saucepan.
She threw it down and leaned on the table.

"Oh, dear. . . . Oh, dear."

At nine o'clock that evening the landlady
knocked at the old woman's door. "Where's
Mrs. Wilson? I haven't seen her all day. Or
the child. I just tried her door, and it's open,
and nobody there."

"Mrs. Wilson? Ah!" The old woman
nodded with the air of one who has a good story.
"Ah! I can tell you. Mrs. Wilson's gone."

" Gone ? "

" Ah! Gone."

" But where to ? What for ? "

" Goodness knows. She's gone. That's all I know. And I got a message for you. She can't find the rent, so she's gone. She's left the things in the room, and wants you to sell 'em. And if there's anything over after the rent, perhaps you'll send it to her when she sends you her address. She's asked me to take care of her box for her. All the rest can be sold."

The landlady looked at the old woman, and then at the door of Jane's room, and then inside the room. She spoke as one presented with the incredible. " Well, I never. Because she hadn't got the rent ? What a fool the woman must be. What-*ever* she do that for ? "

" Now you ask me something. There it is, though. She said she couldn't face you, and she's gone. Her and the little one. Where to, God knows. She had no friends that ever I hear speak of. Anyway, she's gone, and the stuff in there is yours."

" But what a fool. I'd a trusted her for a *month's* rent if she'd asked. And more if she'd wanted it. I know tidy people when I see 'em."

" To be sure. But she's a queer one. I knew

she was in trouble, and I offered to lend her a bit meself. And she nearly blew me head off."

"There now. Did you ever? You do meet some rum ones, don't you?"

Jane was carrying Agatha through the November mud. There was a high wind. Under it the naked naphtha flares of the people's stalls panted. The screened arc-lights of the shops preserved the frigid lustre of a woman in a drawing-room. Jane was tramping to Holland Park against the full rush of it. It got about her skirts and hampered her. It teased her eyes like the thrust of frozen fingers, and slapped her face and disordered her hair. She had but one free hand, and in holding her bonnet to her head she had to let her skirt reach the mud. The thought that her skirt was getting muddy gave her the first full comprehension of her disaster.

Foot by foot, over fields of light and deserts of darkness, she went across the continent of London. She went like a sick animal seeking some corner where it may hide. She was making for the only spot of friendliness that the continent held for her. In all that immensity of trepidation that weaved about her, Amy alone was real and whole. All else was phantasmal, blind and deaf and dumb. She went from the exuberance of the great streets to the quiet precision of the squares, and did not know the one from the other. She tramped past miles of indifferent doors and ice-white windows. She pressed through a pageant of thousands of pale masks. These pale masks were people. They circled and darted upon their separate occasions as though each inhabited the world in solitude. They had no more significance than the bricks of the buildings or the blaze of the lamps. They were just People, as far removed from harmony with her as horses. She went through a forest of tormenting odours. The amber reek of fried-fish shops breathed out of the dark with the intoxication of midnight flowers. A baker's shop gushed the piquant odour of new bread into her face. A restaurant kitchen sent her a sneering hint of tomato soup. These things she noticed. She had not eaten since Friday. Under the brilliant blindness of their windows she began to slink and to seek the lampless patches.

She had a sudden terror that she would not be able to complete the journey; that she would drop down somewhere and die. She tried to avoid the wind by taking side-streets, and twice lost her way. When she discovered for the second time that she had taken the wrong turning, she stopped where she was, and looked for a place to rest. She sat on the stone coping of a front garden, and eased her arm of Agatha's weight. The only phrase she found for her distress was " Oh, dear. . . . Oh, dear."

She was saying this half-aloud when a woman came along. The woman stopped. "What's the matter, ducky? Ain't you well?"

" I'm all right. I'm all right."

" Well, what's the trouble, dearie?"

Jane saw that she was a young woman with a fleering hat. She noted a strong smell of drink, which explained the ducky and dearie. The hat was slightly askew. She sat down by Jane with the air of one ready for an hour's conversation.

" I got to get to Holland Park. I've walked from Piccadilly. And I've got to get to Holland Park. Oh, dear."

" Well, you won't get there this way, ducky. You want to go down there. You'll find a bus there."

" Bus is no good to me."

" How's that, ducky? Eh? Ain't yeh got the fare?"

" No."

" Bless my heart. That's bad. And you walked from Piccadilly. Carrying that big gel, too. Poor thing. Well, well. Look here, lovey, I know what it is to be down meself. Here—you take this—and get a bus. And get yourself a

94

glass o' something warm. This wind goes right through yeh. I had a bit o' luck to-day. And I know what it is." She struggled at the rear of her skirt and brought out a purse. She fumbled with it, and found a shilling. "There—that'll put you on yer way. And good luck to yeh."

Jane stared at the shilling. It had been put so firmly into her hand that she accepted it without protest or thought of protest. A half-awake corner at the back of her drugged mind told her that somebody was being good to her. Somebody she couldn't properly see or comprehend. "I'm sure it's very good of you. I don't know who you are, but it's very good——"

"That's all right, lovey. Tell us the trouble."

Jane put the trouble into a few sentences. "There now. Ain't that rough? Don't some people get lumps of it? I've had enough in my time, I can tell you. But not as rough as yours. Enough to understand, though. Blimey, ain't it cold here?"

"I'm sure it's very good——"

"Don't you worry about that, duck. I had a bit o' luck to-day. And I know what it is. Down that street there, and you'll come to the buses. Keep yer pecker up, Ma. There's better times coming."

"Thank you ever so."

The woman lifted a hand as though about to

cheer. "Gawd—if we can't help each other what're we here for?"

"If I could have your address I could send it back to you when——"

"Send it back be blowed!" The words were a riotous chant of Christian fellowship. "Pass it on, ducky, pass it on. When you get right you're sure to find some other poor soul that's down. Pass it on, and give 'em my love. Good-night, ducky. Gawd bless yer."

She stumbled away and was absorbed into the enveloping purple. Out of it came a witness of her passing—a faint ". . . bless yeh, ducky."

Jane turned back into the wind and reached the main road. As she trudged she thought lovingly of the woman.

In Bayswater Road she stopped a bus. She sat down on the cushions as though she had never sat down before. Her knees were shaking with the strain of the lumpy Agatha. When the conductor held out his hand she asked for Holland Road. He took the shilling and was about to drop it into his bag, and then stopped and looked at it. He held it under the lamp. He bit it. He took out a half-crown and knocked it on the edge of the half-crown. He passed it back to her.

"Somebody's done it on yeh, Ma."

"Eh?"

96

" This is no good. Can't take that."

Faintly she asked " Why not ? "

" 'Cos it's bad."

" Bad ? "

" Yes. Bad. Look at it. That's no shilling. Holland Road threepence."

" A *bad* one ? "

" Yes. Look at it. Can't yeh *see?* Three-pence—Holland Road."

" Oh, dear. That's all I've got."

" Well, can't take that. Sorry."

He rang the bell. The bus stopped.

" Are you *sure* it's a bad one ? "

" Certain. Anyway, I can't risk taking it. So if that's all you got you'll have to get out. Sorry."

" Oh, dear."

" Sorry. There's a lot of 'em about just now. Careful how you go. I'll hand the kiddie out."

The bus rumbled on and left her standing against the railings of Kensington Gardens. She looked forward into the spectral infinity of the great western road. She picked up Agatha and trudged on towards Amy and a sane world.

That night she and Agatha slept in two chairs in the housemaid's pantry of the big house where Amy was cook. Before she slept she spent ten minutes in cleaning the hem of her skirt.

9.

FOR certain choice spirits the crest of Heath Street, Hampstead, was an open-air club. The hearth of this club was the White Stone Pond, and there its youthful members gathered. Their common note was implicit scholarship in the animal side of life, and their talk was an eisteddfod of bawdy. Self-respect compelled them to stagger each other, but each of them, supporting his self-respect by lies, had an uneasy feeling that perhaps the others were not lying. This made them see their own meagre devilries as the arrogance of mice. It forced them to foster bright legend with drab fact, and they came out of the furze bushes of the Heath with tales that would have frozen their fathers' ears.

Conquest was a commonplace, taken for granted among all true males. They did not talk of this. They allowed it to be understood that they were professors of the occult by-paths. They talked of the strange and novel ways by which the conquest was celebrated.

They leaned against the railings opposite the pond. They twirled sticks and canes. They

scanned each girl as she passed, and among themselves they sorted and ranged her as Certain,
Possible, Impossible. Some of the Certain they
knew as willing companions in the furze-bushes.
These, too, they sorted. The students they
dismissed. They asked for savants.

With the crowd came a girl whom three of
them greeted with lifted hats and grins. She
walked serenely. Her face held the reticent pride
of one who feeds on secret bread. Her eyes were
dusky. All the repressed instincts of her father
were loose in her. His bold desire had been
chained by a faint heart. In the daughter bold
desire was abetted by willing heart, and in her
his pale side-glances at gallantry had become
sword-thrust approach and candid fervour. As
she passed she glanced at the boys. By her
glance the novice knew that his secret was open
to her, and the adept knew that he was recognised.

One of them explained her to a new member.
" That's Agatha. Every chap knows her. Now
there's a girl. That's the sort for me. I thought
I knew something, but she knows it all. *All.*
I bet Paris couldn't teach *her* anything."

At fifty-seven Jane was rehabilitated. She was
minding a large house at St. John's Wood while
the owners were travelling, and she was prosper-

ous. She was happy, too; happier than she had been since her first year with Robert. Agatha had grown into a slim and lively girl, and was her good companion. Her liveliness was nicely balanced by sense. She filled the big house with the bright chatter and dancing ways of frivolity, but was always serious enough to help with the cleaning and the washing-up. She had found work for herself, and was managing a newspaper and tobacco shop in Camden Town. She had wages and commission, and was able to buy her own clothes and pay for her food. Her hours were long, and the work was tiring. Jane wondered often how it was that she could be always so bright at the end of a hard day. She put it down to a strong constitution.

She felt that she was indeed blest in her. She was so thoughtful of her mother, and so self-reliant. Jane could trust her anywhere. She knew that all girls wanted a little pleasure, and was glad to let her go to the theatre or for walks with girl-friends. If servants at the other houses wondered that a young girl should be out so late, Jane would tell them that Agatha was old for her years, and not like other girls. She would explain her gaiety and her balance. " I'm sure no mother *could* have a better daughter." She said this every day.

She had brought her up in the light of all that was good, and she was proud of the result. But she did not let her perceive that pride. She never found fault with her, but she held before her examples that no daughter could hope to come abreast of. She showed her how others excelled her in virtue and achievement. The distant view, she felt, would inspire her to develop her goodness to the perfect crescent. Presented with tact, it was better for a young girl than much praise. She thought she was presenting it with tact.

She began to look to the day when Agatha would marry. Being Agatha, she would make a sensible marriage. A man of a higher world than their own, but not too high. She thought of a bank clerk. They were men of character, and their places were fixed. She saw a little villa and garden at Putney, and herself, willingly in the background, nursing her grandson.

At St. John's Wood they were living healthily and delightfully. They had comfortable quarters, and there was a large garden, with fruit trees. Jane was able to dress respectably, to provide good food, and still to save money. When she sat with Agatha in the quiet garden on Sunday afternoons she felt that her struggles had been well rewarded. Amy was dead, and Aunt Sophy was dead. She had no friends at all, but she had

Agatha and she had a good job. She was content. She had come into her haven, where life moved in a sustained adagio. Its tones were rich and full. It looked as though it were now set for a continuance of fair days. Her prayers at night were no longer pleas. They were thanksgivings.

But nothing good stayed long with her. One evening at supper she knew that fair days were ended.

Agatha came to the table in a mood that was not Agatha's. Her face was pale and heavy. She looked at her supper without interest. Jane noted this and gave a quick eye to the supper. She wondered if she had given her something she didn't like. Agatha took a fork and picked at her plate. She ate a mouthful. Then, without further warning of disaster, she dropped the fork and put her hands to her face and became a storm of tears and sobs.

Jane dropped knife and fork and stared. " What on earth——" And then : " Aggie ! What-ever's the——"

In five minutes, each second of which was crystallised misery, she knew.

The fact itself was a bullet shock. For the second time she learned that angels can become devils without altering their form. But after the shock of learning that her Agatha was an elaborate fiction, she thought no more of the fact. She thought only of its reverberations. She forgot that Agatha had ceased to be Agatha. She forgot that her daughter was in distress. She saw only that they were faced with disgrace. However careful you might be, you could never keep this kind of thing quiet. Everybody would know. She saw all her life's battle given away to the enemy. Her own phrase came to mock her— " I'm sure no mother *could* have a better daughter." She heard the hollow laughter of the servants in the near-by houses. She had lost her respectability. She would be a butt for the world's scorn. She was face to face with hell. Because her wound was so deep it was some time before she felt its pain, and a longer time before she could separate the threat of social shame from her grief in the collapse of her virtuous Agatha, and still longer before she could return to the immediate fact that her child was in trouble and needed her love.

She began to ask Agatha questions, but she was not herself and she used the wrong tone. She was shrill and bleak. Agatha too was shrill and bleak. They clashed in quarrel.

She asked, Who? When? How? sharply. Between questions she said to herself, " Oh, God ! . . . Oh, God ! "

Agatha met the questions without grace. " Oh,

never mind. It don't matter. I'm in a mess, that's all. Don't keep saying 'Oh, God!' like that."

"Oh, God! How long's this been going on? Tell me the truth now."

"That time I went to Margate for a week. Fellow I met there. Never seen him since. Don't know where he lives. Anyway, it don't matter. It was my fault as much as his. I'm in a mess, that's all. Thing is, what'm I going to *do*?"

Jane stood over the bowed figure. It was her daughter, but her daughter had outraged the supreme law. She became harder in her judgment of her daughter than she would have been of other daughters, because it was *her* daughter. "Do? Oh, God! I don't know. Enough to make one do away with oneself. Ain't I had enough worry and wretchedness all my life?" There was a sob in her voice.

Agatha became sullen. "Oh, I know I done wrong, but——"

"Bringing shame on me. After all I done. I'm sure I did my best for you."

"I know. . . . I know."

"I've always held me head up. And taught you to."

"Oh, don't *go* for me, when I'm——"

" I'm not going for you. But after all I done.
All the trouble I've had. And then——"

Agatha let out a hysterical laugh in a noise of
" Eurrh." And then in a drumming monotone
—" Don't-nag——don't—don't—nag ! "

The word stung. " *Nag !* I like that. Nagging ! I s'pose I'm to say nothing. Mothers
mustn't say anything to-day. Here have I sacri-
ficed and done without things to bring you up
prop'ly. And then—some fellow at Margate.
Just as though you was a trollop. I'd never
a-thought it of you. If anybody told me——"

" Oh, don't, don't."

" After all I done. After the life I've had.
Always kept meself respectable. And then——"

" Oh, do be quiet. Thing is, what'm I going
to *do ?* "

But Jane couldn't be quiet. She was like a
woman in a burning house arguing about who
started the fire. The word " nag " had struck a
sensitive point. She was concerned with answering injustice. She answered it with unjust sneers.
" What you're going to *do ?* Pity you didn't
think of that last year. Lot of use it is to struggle
to bring your children up nicely. If I'd dragged
you up anyhow, and let you run the streets, I
could understand it. But I brought you up like
a lady. More fool me, I s'pose. Seeing all

you care about it is to go and be a street-walker."

"Oh, go on, go on. Jeer at me." She waved her arms. She was suddenly on the point of screaming. "You seem to a-done all that more for your own pride than for me. I thought mothers were supposed to help their children in trouble, but——"

"Oh, of course, I mustn't say a word. I got to put up with all the shame and disgrace, and then if I say anything I'm nagging."

And then the thundery atmosphere broke into storm and cleared. Respectability said its last word and accepted defeat. Agatha brought her feet to the floor with a smack. She swept a plate off the table. Its pieces made a forlorn tinkle on the oilcloth. She shot up. Her face was a dull flare. "Oh, stoppit, stoppit, stoppit. I'm ill."

The movement and the words did their work. Jane was silenced. She stepped back as from the threat of a hand. They stood posed at each other —tall daughter and small mother. Authority and defiance. Authority had to look up. Defiance looked down. But although the symbolical attitudes were inverted, tradition won. Jane said quietly, "Sit down." Agatha sat down. There were some seconds of silence. The silence healed the bruises of their recrimination. In the same quiet tone Jane said: "If your own child grows up like you, perhaps you'll understand what a mother feels. Perhaps it'll make *you* say things. Now then—let's——"

Agatha, softly weeping, said: "You *made* me fly at you."

It was understood that they were making mutual apology. Each was ashamed. They looked at distant corners of the room. In isolated and personal pain, they wept.

Half an hour later they came together as mother and daughter. Agatha crept to her and put an arm round her. "I'm sorry, Mum. Oh, I'm *sorry* for what's happened. I'm sorry I've hurt you after all you done." Until midnight they talked of ways and means of facing the catastrophe.

Thereafter Jane said no word about disgrace. She saw the duty that had been laid upon her. She accepted the disgrace and performed the duty. She ceased to be a respectable woman holding her head up. She became a mother passionate in service to her child.

She still held her head up to the world, but the strain was great. Her guilty secret destroyed all title to holding her head up, and the lie came hardly to her. She suffered as all honest people suffer in defending false positions. She lived through weeks of dumb and bitter pain. There was the impending Fact, and there was its shadowy regiment of furtive contrivances for concealing it. She had walked a straight road; she was now blundering through a forest.

She took Agatha away from the newspaper shop and kept her indoors. She harboured her as though she were a wanted criminal. She kept her away from windows. She kept her from answering the door. She restricted her to one small corner of the garden which could not be seen from adjoining houses; for once she was seen their shame would be published to the world.

She got a copy of a weekly paper which gave much space to advertisements of discreet lodgings for those who wished to retire from the world for a few weeks. Over a fictitious name she answered three of these advertisements, and arranged a date with a house at Finchley. She bought Agatha a wedding-ring, and explained to the house that the husband was away with his ship. At the appointed time she took Agatha there by night, and returned to her duty as caretaker.

She was summoned three days later. She made a hurried journey by tram and bus. When she reached the house she found Agatha moaning. She met a doctor, who looked unusually grave.

She explained that she was the girl's mother. He nodded.

"'M." Then he said: "I don't want to disturb you, but there's something queer here. With her youth and strength this ought to be an easy affair, but it isn't. It's going wrong. Somebody's been careless. Don't quite like it, but we must wait and see. It may be all right, but you'd better stay."

Fearful of losing her post by neglect of duty, she could only take the risk. That night the St. John's Wood house was left unguarded, and she sat through miserable hours with her daughter.

For the last half-hour she heard nothing but Agatha's voice: "Oh, mum! . . . Oh, mum! . . . Oh, mum!"

In the grey light of six o'clock there was silence.

She went through the funeral and the inquest as a dazed organism. Two months later she could remember only that there had been a funeral and an inquest. She could recall no detail of them nor any of her own actions.

She came slowly back to a realisation of life in a Hampstead hospital. Three months after the death of Agatha she came out of the hospital with no home to go to, no work, no friends, and with two pounds left out of her savings. She found herself a furnished room in a back street of Camden Town. The thought of work weighed upon her body like an iron chain. She felt that even half a day's labour, such as she had once skipped through, would break her. She wanted to cast off the chain, and lie down and rest for ever and ever. But something made her go on.

Ten minutes after she had booked the room she crawled out to look for work.

10.

At sixty-five Jane was cleaning doorsteps in the byways of Shoreditch. It was the last work her failing strength allowed her, and she prayed each night that she might die before her strength was used.

Winter and summer, in frost and fog, she was up and out at seven o'clock. She had once worked for Lady Mellonspar; she was now working for the wives of railway-porters and fish-curers. She earned three-halfpence at each house, and found her own hearthstone. She cleaned steps with the good faith that she brought to all her work. This had given her a regular connection, and by hard and rapid exertion she could just support herself. Her clothes were old and worn, but she kept them and herself as neat as she was able. Her hands were thin, and gnarled by rough labour and much dabbling in warm water. Her knuckles and other joints were getting stiff with threats of rheumatism. Her thick hair had become a few grey strands. The comfortable round face of the St. John's Wood days had become narrow and drawn. Her mouth was a sharp line. It was the mouth of soldiers in the half-hour before retreat.

The women who employed her treated her with some deference. They recognised a something that marked her from other step-cleaners; marked her even from themselves. She was so respectable and well-spoken. The knowledge of this recognition nourished the pride which was her sole strength.

Little food was sufficient for her. Her daily comfort was tea, and once a week she reached at luxury. Every Sunday she treated herself to a glass of stout. Through the six days she saw this glass of stout awaiting her. The prospect of it was a beacon in the week's mist. It was something to work for, and it soothed her work-exhausted nerves.

She had no home. She lived at a women's hostel. This hostel was the effort of a religious body to provide clean lodgings for women who had to do soiling work. It stood in a miserable street off the just-less-miserable Kingsland Road. It was a haven of refuge for the almost-beaten, and it looked more stern than any convict-prison. For one-and-threepence a week she had a cubicle in the first-class dormitory. This cubicle was her world. Her possessions were two bon-

nets, three handkerchiefs, a change of under-
clothing, needles and thread and darning wool,
and a small tin box. The box held her treasure.
In it were the gloves she wore at her wedding,
Agatha's first baby shoes, a photo of Robert,
three photos of Agatha, a photo of Amy, a New
Testament presented on her Confirmation, a
Valentine that Father had sent her, a brooch from
Amy, and the letters of recommendation that
pointed her career of honest work. At nights she
looked through these things and handled them.
She was getting a little queer in her ways.

She did not talk much to the other inmates, but
when they talked to her she was cheerful and
civil. She kept herself to herself, as respectable
people should; and she was respected. On
Wednesday and Sunday evenings there were
prayer-meetings in the Hostel. She attended
these and drew help from them. She liked the
words of the prayers. She did not understand
them all, but they had a comfortable sound.
" Let not your heart be troubled, neither let it be
afraid." " Come unto Me all ye that are weary
and heavy-laden." " The peace of God which
passeth all understanding." They seemed to be
addressed to old people like herself. Sometimes
she felt very old.

On summer evenings she went for lonely rides

on the tram or sat among the social crowd around the bandstand in the park. She liked to look at the flowers in the park, and she liked to watch the young couples courting. At such times she felt that it was good to be alive. On winter evenings she sat with the others in the Common Room. She sat with folded hands and stared at the stove. Most of them sat like that. Most of them could cast back from present winter to green pastures, and throughout the evenings their eyes were turned to those pastures. When they talked their talk was of the long ago. In recalling little outings, and isolated days and hours, they spoke as one speaks of some rapturous moment of religious revelation. Their real world was a world of gracious ghosts, and in the world of present fact they felt themselves to be ghosts. Because of this they talked very little. They sat and stared and turned in their folded hands the ghostly bounty of memory.

Some of them were chair-menders, some were office-cleaners, some sold newspapers or flowers at street-corners. They had nothing to say about their occupations. It was only by chance that this one would discover what that one did. Each morning they went their separate ways into the continent of London, and until the evening they were lost to each other. Pride compelled them to struggle with life in whatever humble corner life allowed them. The same pride made them ashamed of this corner. They were proud to pay their way, but they jealously hid from their world the forlorn makeshifts by which they paid it. In each case it was understood that there had been times when they were fitly set in more reputable work. The wind of misfortune had whirled them from their harmonious setting.

For two years Jane lived in the Hostel. She was supported through those years by a feeling that they were only years of transition; that if she kept steadily at her step-cleaning she must at length reach better times. But her conscious mind told her that she never would. It told her that this was the best she was to know. In dark moments it told her that she might even lose her step-cleaning.

There came a day when she did.

One morning, while she was cleaning steps in Bateman's Row, she fainted. The woman of the house took her to the Hostel, and they put her to bed. She was seen by a doctor, and nursed by one of the Sisters. All she needed, the doctor said, was rest and freedom from worry. That week her employers had to clean their own steps or leave them dirty. The following week they engaged other step-cleaners.

She got the needed rest but not the freedom from worry. While she had her step-cleaning and her cubicle she had life under control. Once she lost them she lost the control; and she knew that life, uncontrolled, was a wild beast. By this enforced absence from work she knew that she would lose her connection, and have to start again. During that fortnight's rest she could do nothing but count money and wonder by what means she could recover her lost work. At the end of the fortnight her tiny store of money was exhausted in the rent of her cubicle and in medicines. She did not dare to think beyond the immediate hour. She could only say to herself: "I never thought I'd come to this. I never thought I'd come to this."

The Sister comforted her with words of praise for her endurance and courage. But she knew that it was the end. She knew it fully when one of the women to whom she had sometimes talked looked in to cheer her with a little gossip.

"How you feeling now, Mrs. Wilson?"

"Oh, I'm middling, thank you. Only tired." The voice was very faint.

"Ah! I hear they're coming for you to-morrow morning."

"Eh?" The voice was sharp.

"Coming for you to-morrow morning."

"Who are?"

"The Relieving Officer."

"The What?"

"The Relieving Officer. I heard 'em arranging it downstairs. Coming for you in the morning. Take you to the Infirmary. You'll be much better off there."

"*Infirmary?*"

"Ah. It'll be much nicer for you there. More comfort, like."

"Oh, God!" Her head rolled on the pillow, as though seeking a way of escape from the world's eye.

"There, now, Mrs. Wilson—don't feel like that. There's more comfort there than here."

"I don't want comfort—not from charity. I only want to pay me way. I don't care how rough it is if I can pay me way. I never taken charity yet."

"Well, we never know what we may come to. None of us."

"I've always worked hard to keep respectable. Goodness knows I've tried." Without shame she wept.

"Yes, but some has the luck and some don't."

"To think that I should come to this."

"I know it's hard when you done your best. But, there——"

"Oh, I can't. I can't. Oh, dear. Oh, dear."
She fumbled for a handkerchief. "Oh, God—to
die in the workhouse. If my father——"

"Well, I got an old friend there, and she says
it's not at all bad. Not nearly what you think.
They have very nice times, I can tell you. And
if you've done your best where's the shame?
Eh?"

"To think that I should come to the workhouse."

"But where's the shame? My friend met
some very nice women there."

"I've done everything I could. I've kept
meself going. And I'm not broken down yet.
But there—I mustn't be a burden on these people.
An' I s'pose I should be if I stayed until I can get
some more work."

"It's much nicer'n this place. They look after
you reely well. And the matron and all the staff
people are reely very nice people, my friend
says."

"When d'you say they're coming?"

"To-morrow morning."

"Oh. To-morrow morning." She appeared
to make a note of this. "I must get meself ready,
then."

"That's right, Mrs. Wilson. Now don't you
be downhearted. You'll find it quite different

from what you think. And as for shame—what about the big ladies that get free lodgings in Hampton Court—eh ? "

"Ah, but that's different. They're Gentry. And Hampton Court——"

" But it's charity, just the same, ain't it ? "

" Ah, you don't understand."

" Well, anything I can get for you ? "

" No, thank you."

" I'll say good-night, then."

" Good-night."

" Good-night. I'll see you in the morning 'fore you go, I expect."

" Yes, I expect so."

But there was no accent of truth in this phrase. As soon as the woman had gone Jane pressed her face into the pillow and tried to think. But she could think little beyond Charity and Workhouse —the twin horrors. If any road led away from them she must take that road. They were coming here for her. The only way of escape was not to be here. So far thought took her, but no farther. She must not be a burden on the hostel. She could not go to the workhouse. Therefore the only thing to do was to get away from the hostel.

She lay in the dark, her mind rolling round this one idea. The fortnight's rest had given her strength, and she murmured a thought of thanks that she was strong enough to get up and go. She waited until all lights were out and the dormitory was silent. Then, as she heard a church clock strike eleven, she got up and dressed. She crept out of the dormitory and down the stairs. She took with her the tin box. There was a back entrance to the hostel, and she sought this and slipped the bolts.

She closed the door softly behind her. Then she stepped out into the dark street and wandered away to find a place to die in.

II.

AT four o'clock of that December morning London lay prone under a bowl of blue-black sky. Its spires and terraces and million-populous streets were merged into a featureless blur. In the moment of inertia between the last of the night's movement and the beginning of the day's, the world's greatest city was still, not in the serenity of reverie or the futility of death, nor in the frozen immortality of statuary; but still as a rushing river arrested and bound in a midland pool. Life hung drooping on a breath.

In squares and side-streets immemorial cats moved like lost souls traversing the interplanetary spaces. They padded the pavements as their fathers padded the earth among the forgotten tombs of Assyria. Here and there one sent into the blue-black its half-human screech. Little leaves made desiccated sounds that lived only as the pulse of silence. Great highways, of fluid character by day, were now no more than regiments of lamps. Policemen stood in archways like effigies of policemen. The shadows o the archways made inaudible thunder against the lamplight.

Across a path of light a spectral figure moved. It loomed bluely against the deeper blue. The lamplight and the moment caught it and isolated it, and transfigured it from a woman carrying a tin box into a symbol of man's pain and man's destiny. By her hint of struggling life she charged the stupor of the city with awe. She was walking to a mental rhythm which had long ceased to express itself to her—"Never thought I should come to this. Never thought I should come to this."

As the night dreamed itself into the day there came, breaking through the frail sphere of sleep, the nibbling and pattering of little mouse-noises. The vast organism shuddered: tiny nerves here and there set its muscles twitching. Engines in the railway depots began to breathe. Engines in the garages began to throb. Horse-carts and lorries put jazz-dirt into the rhythm of the engines. Their headlights turned the purple of the tarmac roads to silver. Acres of roof, emerging from the night, began to reveal themselves as smears of mauve. From their centre rose one pillar of smoke. Out of seven hundred square miles it rose, and, rising solitary from that valley, it held the breathless terror of heathen sacrifice. Ten minutes more, and a hundred other chimneys sent up their pillars; but because they were a hundred they held no mystery. They were the smoking chimneys of houses and shops and hotels indexed in Kelly's London Directory.

Jane saw nothing and heard nothing. She was a wandering spot of life, and her being was a plod. She was walking to find death.

As the clock moved lights began to break from bedrooms and kitchens. The walls of factories and workshops burst into bloom. The bell of a distant fire-engine, rising and declining, drove a yellow arc across the white silence. Over the face of the dead sky passed a hand of life. The blue-black horizon was pierced by a green spear. With imperceptible pace the cleft widened and became a wedge of zinc, and with imperceptible pace the wedge forced its way into the blue-black. The keen air of the night took a flavour of acid. The blue-black was fretted away, and the zinc broadened into patches of the green light that lives on the sea's bed, and the morning star died. It was the birth of a new day, and it carried all the sour agony of the moment before birth.

Under these sepulchral hues, and through the cold murmurs of the aroused sluggard, she plodded, looking for a secret place where she might make her end. But not even the appalling magnitude of London could afford a secret place. Even these evacuated hours held wanderers like herself, and wherever she sought secrecy she found the threat of company. She learned on this walk that London is never forsaken. As the conquerors retire, the defeated come out and take ghostly possession. She plodded on.

Slowly the octopus heaved and awakened. Its long, chilly fingers began to crawl with life. Minute by minute the little crepitations multiplied and took volume, until they became one faint noise of the quality of muted 'cellos. Cats made their last prowl among the dust-bins. Street-cleaners made their last strokes of brush and broom; domestics made their first strokes. Milkmen began the delivery of a million bottles of milk. Boys dropped newspapers at a million doors. Watchmen, their eyes without lustre, tramped home to bed, and met early workers, lustreless too, going laggingly to factory gates. Charwomen carried bent life into the sterile streets about the Bank and Mansion House. Severe clubs of St. James's opened their doors to the ignoble, and the ignoble made them sweet and clean for the cunning and the fortunate. The fifteen great roads that lead from the five counties to the inner circle of London began to twinkle with faces.

From ten thousand chimneys now the smoke drawled into the air. The dolorous cry of the sweep was its voice. Its blue mixed with the morning green, and turned the sky sick. One by one the street lamps gasped and died, and the lights from factories and kitchens winked out. Bus and tram shot their fleets into the highways. Other instruments joined the orchestra, and soon it was churning and fomenting in its tuning-up for the symphony of day. Teams of figures from the railway stations began to surge about the buses. They wore in their eyes and mouths the strained lines of the athlete. They engaged in a battle of ants. They fought their opponents with hips and elbows. The course and detail of their lives were directed by a dead force called Work. All who hindered their obedience to it were their foes.

Jane plodded on. And, as she plodded, in every ten minutes the face of the sky changed from zinc to pearl, from pearl to primrose, and from primrose to gold; until at last over the valley rode the father of all beauty—Light. It drew from dark towers the sheen of silver, and golden fire from pinnacle and cross. One by one it picked them out, lighting here and here and here, adding stanza upon stanza to the completion of the poem of might and majesty which man has made and called London.

In this moment of full sunburst there was a scurry, and Jane joined it. With the coming of light the mean and pitiful things of the dark began to creep back into their holes. For the conquerors it was dawn and life. For *them* it was night and retirement. In every street one of them could be seen. About them was an inrush of eager movement, but they did not look at it. They did not look at each other. Like wounded animals they kept as far from their kind as they could. Because they had nowhere to go, they moved with a resolute air of going somewhere. Those who saw Jane would have said that she was keeping an overdue appointment. She was.

She had walked away to die. But in that night walk she had learned that she could not die. At first she could not die because she could not find a place to die in. Later, when she found the river and solitude, something seemed to shout *Sin!* She was ready to die, and she had no fear of the dreadful minute; but it seemed that God wouldn't let her die. With each thought of the act, and each preparation for it, came this something that told her she was a coward. It was something too slow and vague to be called a revelation, but it was something that did bring with it a change of feeling. With the coming of the sun she knew that she must not do this

126

thing. To die was to run away from trouble, and never yet had she run away from trouble At the end of her grinding plod she had learned that it was shameful to be ashamed of shame. She had failed : that was all; and she must drop her flag of pride and accept the shame as she had accepted the struggle.

None of this came to her by thought. It was slowly pressed into her, and her weakness took its impress without contest. She knew now that she must accept. And with this knowledge came happiness. In that moment life yielded the secret which men vainly pursue by struggle. The moment she ceased to struggle she was clothed in a blessed peace.

She was in this mood of acceptance when a hand fell on her arm. In her flight from the hostel she had thought that by walking on and on she would get farther away from it; but in all her walk she had seen only pavement and road. She did not know that she had come full circle. She was in Kingsland Road when the hand touched her and the strong womanly voice said, " Well, sister." For a moment she was startled; then she answered the voice with a smile. " Come sister. Where have you been all night ? We've been looking for you. We were afraid that something had happened."

" I went for a walk. To think things out. I was going to do something wrong. But I'm better now."

" That's good, sister." A pale, kind face looked out of a black poke bonnet, and a firm hand took her arm.

She allowed herself to be led away and washed and fed. Next morning she allowed herself to be led to the workhouse. A group of the hostel inmates went with her.

AT the gates of the workhouse the Sister left her with her escort. It was three days before Christmas. The air was dry and brisk. There was sharp sunshine.

"Be of good heart, sister. God is with you. His glory is everywhere. This is the season when the Blessed Lamb was sent to redeem us. Be of good heart."

"I will, dear, I will."

"Praise Him!"

The women gathered round her with condoling words. At this closing of her days she tried to draw up from memory the things that had happened to her. But they would not come. She could draw only threads. In a coloured procession came dripping-toast, the cows of Steeple End, bells across the evening fields, Christmas balloons, Robert's imitation of Lord Wolseley, Agatha tumbling out of her high chair, the pears she had picked in the St. John's Wood garden, the entrance hall of the Majestic, a Band of Hope tune, a good tea she had had at Hampton Court with Amy. . . . The procession went across her eyes like a jerked ribbon. Then she turned to the circle of condolence.

"Well, good-bye all. And thanks for seeing me off." The holiday phrase came unwittingly. The next phrase did not. She was retiring from the world, taking the veil of defeat. It seemed that the occasion should be pointed. They were waiting for her to point it. She searched about, and then from some overlooked corner she snatched a little dried pea that was all that remained of the fluent courage that had served her for sixty years.

"Well, there's one thing: I shall have a good rest for once."

The touch of humour eased their restraint and they broke into free laughter at the old woman's drollery. They armoured her with laugh and talk.

"You'll have a good Christmas dinner, any-way."

"Yes, I shall have a good Christmas dinner."

"You'll be able to come and see us on your day out."

"Yes, I shall be able to come and see you. Perhaps some time one of you'll come and see me."

"To be sure we will. We'll come and see

you. We'll see if we can't bring you something nice."

" There now. Isn't that kind ? . . . Well, I've had some happy times. Perhaps I shall still."

" Course you will."

" I never been in debt. I never been in a pawnshop. And till now I've never had parish relief. I've always paid me way. Always held me head up."

" And so you can now, Mrs. Wilson. So you can now. You can hold your head up with the best of 'em."

" Yes, I s'pose I can. Why not ? I've always done me best. I might a-died before I come to this, but I didn't. Perhaps God knows best. Perhaps He wanted me to see what a good time I'd had. Isn't it a lovely day ? Makes you feel glad to be alive."

" Yes, don't it ? "

" Well, good-bye all."

" Good-bye, Ma."

She went through the gates.

In the narrow street, squalid with December mud, children were playing as she had played outside the workhouse at Clerkenwell. They, too, would grow up. They, too, would pass through travail and trouble, and bear children, and die without knowing why they had lived, and without leaving any sign that they need have lived. Jane was at the end of it. They were at the beginning. But the tale would be the same : an unconstructed blur of pain and joy and inertia; and at the end, where the solution should be— Nothing. Nothing to show that they need ever have lived. Nothing, that is, save the fragrance of the flower of life crushed in their closed hands.

Life is a novel dreamed by God in a garden and never written. We are its characters, and our tale is never fully told. Because of this we are fretful. At the end we feel that this is not the end, that we have not fulfilled ourselves. But it may be that the only fulfilment asked of us, scholar and saint and simple, is that we shall catch the fragrance of that garden, and find it beautiful. It may be that there is but one sin that for ever shuts the sinner from the friendship of God—to mock this garden of rose and thorn, and call it a mire.

As Jane walked into the workhouse the fragrance of this garden went with her.